EVERYBODY IN TOWN KNEW LILL HODSDEN, AND MOST OF THEM HAD A MOTIVE TO KILL HER....

Her mother was murderously mad at Lill's lack of morals.

Her steady lover was sick to death of being black-mailed.

Her neighbors were dying to get even with her.

Her daughter's boyfriend would do anything to stop her from reporting him to the immigration officials.

Her sons were determined to put an end to her over-bearing ways.

Her lover's invalid wife had developed a killer's instinct about her husband's tawdry affair.

And since the rest of the townsfolk wanted to give the murderer a medal, Chief Inspector Dominic Mc-Hale found himself stumped on his very first homicide case—puzzled by a lengthy list of likely suspects and a very clever killer.

SCENE OF THE CRIME® MYSTERIES

MURDER INK® MYSTERIES

A Scene Of The Crime® Mystery

DEATH
of a
PERFECT MOTHER

Robert Barnard

A DELL BOOK

Published by
Dell Publishing Co., Inc.
1 Dag Hammarskjold Plaza
New York, New York 10017

The lines from "Lily the Pink" in Chapter 2 are quoted
by permission of the Noel Gay Music Company Ltd.

Dell ® TM 681510, Dell Publishing Co., Inc.

ISBN: 0-440-12030-6

Reprinted by arrangement with Charles Scribner's Sons

Printed in the United States of America

First Dell printing—September 1982
Second Dell printing—July 1983

CHAPTER 1

MOTHER AND SONS

Clip-clop down Carnation Road on her way to the shops went Lillian Hodsden, in the last week of her mortal life.

'Hello, Mr Davies. How's the lumbago? Better? Bet you're glad Spring is here, eh? That'll buck you up.'

Mr Davies, tottering home in the opposite direction, let out an ambiguous grunt intended to signify that, thank you for asking, it was no better, and in his opinion Spring was not here, nor even on its way. But he needn't have bothered even with that minimal response. Lillian Hodsden had clomped past him, oblivious, her eye fixed on the next recipient of her early morning cheeriness.

'Hello, Mrs Wharton. Lovely day. Saw you'd got your daughter down. That's nice. And the kiddies? Oh, lovely. Give them a kiss from me, won't you?'

At the mention of the grandchildren Mrs Wharton had shown signs of wanting to stop, but Lillian Hodsden would have nothing of it: having no grandchildren herself, thank God, she was unable to bore back in kind, so she shrilled: 'Can't stop. Got all the weekend shopping to do. Can't think where the weekdays go to, can you?' and she cantered ahead, leaving Mrs Wharton with vague feelings of rebellious irritation, for she was a widow lady who found her time, minute by minute of it, all too easy to account for. She looked round, eyes narrowed, at the diminishing form of Lillian Hodsden.

It wasn't a form you'd mistake easily. Lill was forty-eight but it needed no more than a dash of generosity to suggest forty-two. Buttoned tight round her chunky, bullet-breasted body was a leopard-skin coat, skimpy in proportions but flagrant in falsity. On her feet were a pair of cheap sandals, shiny black edged with gold braid, with heavy wooden heels that made rhythmic patterns on the stony tarmac, announcing her coming as surely as if she were Carmen practising with her castanets in the wings. Crowning the whole effect—and no one could deny that she did make an effect—was a mop of copper-red hair, blatantly untrue to nature, and looking as if she had just dipped her head in a sink full of bull's blood.

You noticed Lill Hodsden, people said in Todmarsh.

Lill was not a native of the undistinguished little southwestern seaside town where she had made her home. She had come here from Leicester in the early 'fifties, the years when Tory freedom was giving people vague yearnings: sniffing the air they smelt money, undreamed-of comforts, the chance of a quick financial kill. It was a time for mobility, geographical and social. Lill Hodsden had her eyes on both. We weren't good enough for her, her neighbours in the Midlands said when she left, and once she'd gone back to tell them they were right.

So she—and incidentally a husband, and incidentally a baby boy—had migrated to the South in search of richer pastures: a classier-sounding address; a nicer type of neighbour; schools with better names and more impressive uniforms. She never asked whether she would be accepted, any more than she listened to the replies to her casually flung cheerinesses. She was Lill, and good as the next woman. Over the years she had acquired two more children, and brought her mother down to live next door, but otherwise than that she did not change. Her neighbours it was who finally had to swallow the outrageously sugared pill. She had settled in this dull little town like a bird of exotic (albeit artificial) colouring alighting on a hen-coop. Finally the hens had had to treat her as one of themselves, though they never ceased to look bewilderedly at the plumage.

Her early morning shopping, today and every day, was a royal progress from butcher's to grocer's, from grocer's to greengrocer's. Everywhere she was known. Everywhere she had her standard little jokes and greetings. Everywhere, she was sure, she was loved. For Lill Hodsden was quite unconscious of the possibility that she made any impression other than the one she intended. 'Quite a character, our Lill,' she'd once heard the greengrocer say. She had taken it as a seventy per cent-proof compliment. She *was* quite a character. She had a cheery wave for everyone, knew everybody's history, opinions and little ways, and had the appropriate words of greeting for each one of them.

'They all say I'm a marvel,' she would tell her family. 'They don't know how I do it.'

So today she clattered from establishment to establishment, exchanging ear-singeing salutations with the other customers, chatting along in her high-speed-drill voice as she waited her turn, chaffing the butcher's boy or the grocer's wife with her age-old jokes and meaningless saws when at last she got to the counter.

'Mind you give us a good bit, Bert,' she shrilled to the butcher, gazing with ignorant vagueness down at the offered choice (for she could no more tell a good piece of meat from a bad one than she could tell a sparrow from a chaffinch). 'It's my Gordon's birthday Sunday, and he does like a good joint. None of your fatty bits, now.'

'Not on your life, Lill,' said Bert, with the forced grin that many faces assumed when confronted by Lillian Hodsden. 'More than my life's worth. I wouldn't dare.'

'Nor I don't believe you would,' said Lill, with a cackle of self-approbation. 'I've got *him* where I want him, eh?' and she turned to her audience to exact homage.

The newsagent was the recipient of her lengthiest confidences. She dropped in at the end of her tour, her shopping baskets laden with meat and groceries, vegetables and out-of-season fruit, plonked them down on the floor, picked up *Weekend* and *TV News,* and proceeded to take over the shop.

'Isn't it a lovely day? They laid it on just for me, you know. They like me up there. It's my Gordon's birthday tomorrow. I'm going to do him proud. Here, have you got a big box of chocks? Something real swank? Let's have a look, then.'

She grabbed the proffered boxes—large and plush, large and garish—in her pudgy hands and carefully picked the most expensive. (Where does she get the money from? thought the newsagent—a rhetorical thought if ever there was one, for he had a very good idea.)

'Nothing but the best, eh?' resumed Lill, slapping down the money. 'You're not twenty-six every day of the week!'

'What's your Gordon doing now?' asked the news-agent, without any great curiosity.

'At this moment I'd guess he's lying in bed,' said Lill, with her parrotty laugh. 'That's where they were when I come out, both the boys. I shouted up to them, I said: "You be out of there before I come back, or you'll feel my hand on your b.t.m's!" Oh, we do have a laugh, me and the boys. They're lovely lads, both of them.' She opened the door into the watery sun-shine, a South of England apology for a fine day. 'We think the world of each other,' she said. 'They'd do anything for me.'

'She'll have to be got rid of,' said Gordon Hodsden, lying on his frowsty bed, puffing at a cigarillo and looking up at the ceiling. 'Some way or other, she's got to be put down.'

His brother Brian, lying on the bed by the op-posite wall, turned his book on to its face on the bedside table and said: 'What do you think she's say-ing at this moment?' His voice took on the authentic parakeet shrillness: ' "Have you got a nice plump chicken for Sunday dinner, Bert? Mind it's a good one, because—" '

Here Gordon joined in the chorus: ' "—my Gordon he does like a nice bit o' breast!" '

The bedroom rocked as they both shrilled a mother-ly squawk of laughter.

' "You've gotta laugh, haven't you?" ' resumed
Brian, unable to give up the routine. ' "Makes the
world go round, a bit of laughter, I always say. We
have some good laughs, me and the boys." ' He lowered his voice to a confidential pitch that was somehow just as false and unpleasant: ' "But they're lovely
boys, both of them. They think the world of me. Worship the ground I walk on. They'd do anything for
me, they would, my Gordon and Brian." '

'The question is, *what* shall we do for her, or rather
to her?' said Gordon, lying back on the bed, his brown
cigarillo pointing upwards to the ceiling, wreathing
himself in smoke. 'Or, to put it bluntly, how are we
going to do her in?'

Brian too lay back on his bed in rapt, companionable contemplation, though the close observer might
have noticed the tiny furrow on his young forehead,
the trouble in his blue eyes. Physically there was no
great likeness between Lill's two boys. Gordon was
tall and chunky, with a mop of dark hair, and work-
ing-man's shoulders and hands. His face was good-looking enough, but restless and instinct with a half-under-
stood aggression. He had had five years in the army,
had bought himself out with Lill's help, and was now
working at the local shipyard—and the fact that she
felt this was not 'good' enough for him was one reason
why his mother had not answered the newsagent's en-
quiry as to what he was doing now.

His brother Brian was nineteen, so his half-formed
look was more understandable. He was slight, fair, and
in his pyjamas looked no more than a boy. He too
was restless, with the restlessness of feared failure, of
chafing against something he knew he was not strong
enough to fight. He was aiming, uncertainly, at uni-

versity. What Gordon and Brian had in common was their manacle and chain. Physically they were as different as chalk and cheese, and Lill would certainly have made jokes about their paternity if she could have done so without impugning their legitimacy. Nothing like that was to be said about either of her boys! On the subject of her daughter she had no such inhibitions.

'The great thing about Mum,' said Brian eventually, 'about Lill, sweet songbird of the Midlands, our beloved giver of life—the great thing about her is her regularity.'

'Oh Christ, don't mention her bowels,' said Gordon, turning over in his bed in disgust, and cursing as his cigarillo stubbed itself out in the pillow.

'Not her bowels, you clot, her habits. Her beastly habits. She generally does everything she does at the same time. Especially of an evening.'

Gordon, engaged in brushing the ash off his bed, and turning over the pillow, on which a tiny burn-hole had appeared, paused. 'You're right,' he said. 'Regular as clockwork. Everything according to plan. Down the pub at seven-fifteen, back from the pub at nine-thirty. It's all part of her shattering predictability. It's one of the things that make her—'

'So utterly loathsome to live with. Agreed. The fact that even when she's out and you've got a bit of rest from her, you keep looking at the clock, knowing that on the dot she'll breeze in and say: "Yoo-hoo. I'm home! How's my boys? Had a lovely evening, have you?" Right you are. Still, it has its uses.'

'When you are planning to do her in,' said Gordon.

'Right. When you are planning to put an end to an existence that brings joy to none, and irritation, nausea, fear, loathing and actual physical vomiting to thousands.' Brian rolled the words round his mouth lovingly. Words were his refuge, his secret, solitary defence. The only way he could tolerate Lill being Lill and being his mother was to form the words that described her. He lay on the bed forming more phrases, a thesaurus of hate, while Gordon began his morning liturgy of exercises—press-ups, running on the spot, lithe swoops of the trunk from side to side and violent feints at this and that. Gordon's regular exercises were a relic of his army days, something he clung to as desperate men do cling to sure things as they sink in oceans of uncertainty. Besides, as he often said, you never knew when training might come in useful.

'Bloody Tarzan,' said Brian, tired with all the activity. 'Give over and think.'

'I am thinking,' said Gordon, back on the floor and pressing himself up and down at double speed with an expert judgment that just stopped him bashing his chin against the floor. 'This is when I do think.'

'Funny brain you must have,' said Brian. 'What's the result of your thinking?'

Gordon stopped, swivelled himself round on to his haunches, and sat looking at his brother's bed, his square shoulders hunched forward urgently.

'Saturday. That's the result of my thinking. Saturday. One week from today. As she's coming home from the pub. A sharp blow on the back of the head as she comes through Snoggers Alley. Or maybe a rope round her throat. Are you with me?'

' 'Course I'm with you.' Brian lay back against his pillow, his weaker, less intense face wreathed in smiles. 'What an idea! They'll think it's some casual mugger, eh? We'll take her handbag and keep the small change.' He drowned in ecstatic anticipation. 'Wouldn't it be marvellous?'

Gordon threw himself forward on to his brother's bed and shook him by the shoulders: 'Stupid bastard! It's not a case of "wouldn't it!" I'm serious!'

Brian looked at him, half wondering, half afraid. 'Serious? You mean you . . . you mean we could?'

'I mean we've got to. I mean it's our only chance. What else is there? I tried, didn't I—tried to get away. I went into the army, got away for five years. Only it wasn't away at all. Everywhere I went I had this ball and chain attached, labelled "Lill". It'll be the same with you. Why did you fail your Scholarship levels? Because deep down you wanted to. And she wanted you to too. Now there's no question of Oxford or Cambridge. That would have taken you away from Lill, from old Dracula curls. Now the best you can hope for is South Wessex—twelve miles of good motorway and back home for tea with Lill at five o'clock. Just what she planned for all along.'

' "They say it's very good for Socialology," ' quoted Brian with a bitter smile.

'You'll have the ball and chain on, boyo, same as I felt in the army. And it'll be there as long as she's alive, and when she dies there'll be no life left in us because we'll have been sucked dry. To get rid of that chain we've got to snap it off.'

'If only . . .' said Brian, faltering.

'What?'

'If only there were some other way.'

'There isn't!' Gordon towered over him, pumping him full of his own energy. 'If a getaway was possible I'd have made it. But I came back, and you'll be stuck here for life. I got the job at the shipyard—and we all know how I got that—and you'll go to our little neighbourhood university and land a job as a teacher in some local dump. And that's our lives. *All* our lives. Lill in the centre of her web, entertaining her flies.'

'You might get married . . . I might too.'

Gordon's face darkened. 'Do you think I haven't thought about that? In fact that's . . . But it couldn't happen while Lill's alive. Oh, I've got girl-friends all right, plenty of them, but anything more than that? I couldn't. As long as she's there I couldn't . . .'

'There's a book about that—*Sons and Lo*—'

'This isn't a fucking book! Sod your books! It's my life! And if I went to . . . her, if I made her want me, what would happen? We set up home in this town, and I'm still mother's boy. We go away, and I'm on a longer lead, same as in the army. She's got us, body and soul. She's owned us, every minute of our lives since the day we were born. If we ever get free, it'll be violently—it'll be by doing her in.' He stared down at his brother. 'Are you with me?'

Brian didn't look up. 'Who is she?'

'What the hell are you talking about? Answer me.'

'Who is it you want to marry?'

'Ann Watson up the road, if you must know. She hasn't so much as looked at me. Why should she? Poor old Gordon Hodsden, the big milksop: still tied to his mother's apron-strings at his age. Before she'll ever look at me I've got to be free. Come on, give me an answer. Are you with me?'

Brian's heart seemed to stop still, then to leap exultantly in his slight body. 'Yes!' he said. Then he turned to his brother and said 'Yes, yes, yes!'

'All right then,' said Gordon. 'Now we can get down to business.'

'The trouble is,' muttered Brian, suddenly abstracted again, and pushing a lock of fair hair back from his forehead in worried frustration, 'that the family's always suspected first.'

'The *husband's* always suspected first,' said Gordon. 'Old Fred. Can you see old Fred doing our Lill in? Can you visualize it? He'd have to ask permission first. Anyway, Saturday night's his night on the town. His night out on parole. Darts at the Yachtsman's Arms. He's bound to have twenty people to swear he was down there being the life and soul of the party every minute from eight to ten-thirty.'

'In which case,' said Brian, 'they'll look at us.'

'Why should they? Us? Her beloved boys? We're one big happy family. The whole town knows that. Lill and her lads. We worship the ground she walks on.' Gordon came up and sat on Brian's bed, looking at him closely. 'You ever told anybody, Bri?'

'What do you mean?'

'Told anybody what we feel? About Lill? How she makes goose pimples go up and down our spine every time she opens her bloody mouth? How we'd like to put her guts through a mincer? Shut her in a slow oven and listen to the howls? Have you told anyone?'

There was silence for a minute. 'No. I never have,' said Brian, swallowing hard. 'It's not—the kind of thing you say, is it? I mean, nobody at school talks much about their mothers. And anyway—I mean, when she goes around, saying what she does—'

'Spreading the gospel of light—the Hodsdens, mother and sons, as the apostles of cheery family togetherness. Exactly. Everyone knows we're devoted. Lill has told them so. She thinks so herself. She's given us our let-out. She's dug her own grave.'

Brian smiled, slowly. 'That's nice. It seems—appropriate.'

'Too bloody right it is. Now all we've got to do is think through the details.'

Downstairs a door banged. 'You lads still up there, wasting a lovely day like this?' carolled the crow voice from downstairs. 'You shift yourselves or I'll be up there with a broomhandle.' And she burst into affectionate laughter.

'Coming, Mum, just getting dressed,' came the duet from the bedroom. But as they scrambled into their clothes Brian took Gordon by the arm and whispered: 'I've just remembered. That book. *Sons and Lovers.* He did his mother in there, too.'

'Bully for him,' muttered Gordon. 'I didn't think we'd be the first. How did he do it?'

'Drugs. She was ill already.'

'That's no good. Lill's got the constitution of a horse. It's got to be some other way. Think about it.' He suddenly took Brian by the shoulders and pushed him against the wall. 'You do agree, don't you?' he hissed, looking into his eyes. 'It's the only way. She's got to be killed.' Brian, wondering, nodded. 'All right then. Now we've got to decide on the way.'

As they pushed in the tails of their shirts and pulled on their shoes they both were turning over in their minds various delicious possibilities.

CHAPTER TWO

FAMILY NIGHT OUT

It's a rehearsal. That's what it is, a rehearsal, thought Brian. This is how it's going to be, one week from today. And one week from today Lill will get her chips, hand in her cards, bite the dust, go to meet her (much to be pitied) Maker. This is a trial run for her murder. I've got to keep my wits about me; observe everything; notice possibilities—things we could take advantage of, pitfalls that could arise. I can't just switch off like I usually do. I'll have to keep on the *qui vive*.

It was very much a family night out. They were celebrating Gordon's birthday a day early—because, as Lill said, Sunday night in a pub's dead as a doornail. So as usual they had gone down to the Rose and Crown (even the pub names in Todmarsh were unimaginative) as they did every Saturday. They had as always taken the side way, through the little cutting known popularly as 'Snoggers Alley', and then down Balaclava Road. Their whole route was vilely ill-lit—providentially, wonderfully ill-lit, Brian had whispered to Gordon. Six and a half minutes ordinary walking time, Gordon had said as they opened the door to the Saloon Bar. Gordon was very consciously the technician of the enterprise.

Now they were all seated round a table, and beyond the fact that Lill had flaunted up to the bar and announced 'It's my Gordon's birthday, so we'll expect a free round later on,' and then had turned to the sparse collection of early evening drinkers and shrilled, 'Get yourselves in good voice for "Happy Birthday To You" later on'—apart from that, it was a normal Saturday night out for the Hodsdens.

Well, almost. Because tonight Fred was with them, just for a first pint, and just to be friendly, like. Fred invariably played darts at the Yachtsman's Arms on Saturday nights, but tonight he raised his glass to his elder son and looked with satisfaction around his little table. Fred was thin, decidedly wizened, and very quiet. Almost humble, you might say. He was like a plant that had never quite flourished after transplanting. Here he was, still pottering round the town's parks as a basic wage gardener twenty-odd years after they had moved to Todmarsh. Happy enough, in fact, but hardly prosperous, and looking all of twenty years older than his wife. It was not quite what Lill had envisaged when she'd made the move. She told him often enough that he ought to consider himself bloody lucky she'd married him, and indeed that was exactly what in his own mind he did feel. He agreed with his wife absolutely.

She's a real winner, my Lill, he thought, raising his mug to his lips. Regular life and soul of the party. And she's brought up a wonderful family. I'm a lucky man.

Lill Hodsden's daughter was also out with the family tonight and drinking a gin and lime. She was an occasional rather than a regular addition, and as a matter of fact she was still well under eighteen. But what landlord would argue the toss with Lill? Come to that, what policeman? So tonight Deborah tagged along with Mum and the boys because until later she had nothing better to do.

Deborah she had been christened (C. of E., what else?), Debbie she had become. She hated the name in both forms. It symbolized Lill's classy aspirations, and their shoddy outcomes. Mary, Eileen, Dorothy would have been better. Or even, come to that, Petula or Cilla. But she was Deborah, become Debbie. She heard her mother speaking:

'Look at old sourpuss over there. Come on, give us a smile, Debbie . It doesn't cost you anything. It's Gordon's birthday, what do you think we brought you out for? Get a smile on your dial, fer Chrissake.'

Lill disliked her daughter. For a start she wasn't a boy, and Lill preferred boys—well, didn't everyone? Then, in the last year, she had grown up, so on family outings there they were together, mother and grown-up daughter, thirty-odd years all too evidently between them. They were like two pages in a family snap-album, wide apart. Only Deborah had all the looks that Lill had had as a girl, without any of the coarseness. She hasn't got a *bit* of my go! said Lill to herself, consolingly.

If I can only get away from her, thought Debbie to herself, nothing in my life can ever be as bad again. If I can only get shot of Lill . . .

'Well, we won't let old sauerkraut cast a blight over the proceedings,' said Lill, turning back to her boys. 'This place seems to need a bit of pepping up tonight. I can see I'll have to brighten things up with a few verses of "Lily the Pink" later on. That'll put a firework up them.'

Oh God, thought Gordon, not Lily the Pink. I don't think I could stand it. It's *my* birthday. Why should *my* birthday be celebrated with 'Lily the Pink'?

For even Gordon didn't quite realize that it was *his* birthday, but Lill's celebration.

Luckily Lill's attention was distracted for the moment by the arrival of Mr Achituko.

'Archie!' she trilled. 'It's my pal! Yoo-hoo, Archie!' For Lill, never very good on words of over three syllables, had been totally defeated by Achituko and had picked on Archie as friendly-sounding. Mr Achituko, his smile fixed and imperturbable, wished he had gone into the public bar, or to the King's Head, or back to the Coponawi Islands. But as always happened with Lill, he gave in to his fate and brought his glass over to the table by the Hodsdens. He was greeted by Lill as manna from Heaven. He was something to enliven her evening.

'It's my boy-friend. Isn't he lovely? I could eat him.' Instead of which she kissed him loudly, for the benefit of the whole bar. Then, as she always did, she regarded his blackness comically, and said: 'Does it rub off?'

Mr Achituko smiled—fixedly, imperturbably. Debbie flushed and looked at the table. Fred, watching out of his washed-out blue eyes like aged overalls, said to himself: My Lill's in great form. Always gets a bit of fun going. Just what this place needs.

Darts were Fred's treat of the week, but when he

drained his glass and stood up, it was almost with reluctance.

'Well, I'd better be off,' he said. 'Enjoy yourselves.'

'Okee-doke,' said Lill, off-hand. Fred threaded his
way apologetically through the drinkers, and as she
heard the door-latch click after him, Lill beamed
round at her brood and said: 'Well, he doesn't leave
much of a hole, does he?'

And it was true. That was the trouble with so
many of Lill's brutalities. They were true, or horribly close to target at worst. When Fred had left
the room you couldn't remember whether he had a
moustache or not, whether he wore glasses or not. He
left behind himself nothing much more than a vaguely
snuffed-out atmosphere and a smell of old clothes.

And now, thought Brian, this really is a rehearsal.
This is how it will be next Saturday. Just Gordon
and me, Debbie perhaps, and Lill. Debbie will go before long, because she can't stand being out with
Lill for more than an hour or so. She'll drift off to
see one of her friends. She'll be sure to be somewhere
where there are people to swear to her presence. Just
as there'll be people here, in this pub, to swear to us.

' 'Ere, look,' said Lill in a stentorian whisper, 'look
who's over there. It's that little Mrs Watson from
along the road. Isn't that good? She's such a lovely
girl. Sort of distant . . . aristocratic, know what I
mean? She shouldn't shut herself away like she has
been. She must be getting over it at last.'

In the far corner of the bar, sitting with a girl-
friend, was a woman in her mid-twenties. She had
long fair hair, an unmade-up face with classically

perfect features, and eyes full of pain. Distant she
may have been, but she registered Lill: a twitch of the
mouth, a fleeting expression of annoyance, showed
she was aware of Lill's interest. She leaned forward
over a bag of potato crisps, talking with desperate
concentration to her friend.

'Do you know,' said Lill, still in that same ear-
shattering whisper, and leaning across to Mr Achituko
in hideous intimacy, 'her husband was killed in
Northern Ireland. Shot in the back. On duty. Isn't it
awful?'

'Yes, I know,' said Mr. Achituko, his fixed smile
disappearing for a moment. 'I have talked with her.'

'Oh, have you?' said Lill, withdrawing in dis-
pleasure. 'Well, don't you go trying to cut out our
Gordon. I've got her marked down for him.'

'Stow it, Mum,' said Gordon, who had flinched
when the name was first mentioned but now responded with great geniality: 'I can choose my own
girl-friends.'

'Well, you've never chose half such a smasher as
that yet,' said Lill. 'She's just what you need. She's
just coming out of her shell too—it's taken her quite
a time.' A thought struck her. 'Crikey, if old Fred
snuffed it I'd be on the look-out for my next on the
trip back from the cemetery.'

She had forgotten her whisper, and bellowed it
round the whole bar, looking complacently at the people at the surrounding tables. One of them said: 'I
bet you would, too, Lill,' and she chuckled in self-
approbation.

Getting serious again, she turned to Gordon and
said: 'Why don't you go and chat her up a bit, Gord?
She's a lovely girl, just your style. You ought to get

to know her better, it's only neighbourly.' And she winked suggestively. Lill prided herself on not keeping her boys tied to her apron-strings. She was always telling them to go out and get themselves girls. Mrs Watson would make a lovely wife for her Gordon. She'd be a better housewife than most, having been married before. And he'd be living just up the road.

'Come off it, Mum,' said Gordon, with that unabated good-humour that now, more than ever, it was essential to preserve. 'What would I say to her? "My Mum says I was to come over and chat you up a bit"?'

'Oh, go on with you. You've got more nous than that. You can do it casual, like.'

Gordon smiled enigmatically, but when five minutes later he went to the bar, he exchanged a few cheery words with little Mrs Watson from along the road. And Lill, pointy ears aquiver, caught them, purred, and smiled at Brian a smile of (she thought) great subtlety, full of hidden meaning.

Don't smirk at me, you old crow, thought Brian. You've got us all on a puppet-string, haven't you, or so you think? Just a little twitch from those pudgy, purple-painted fingernails and we jerk up and do your bidding. In one week's time, oh horrendous Lill, you are going to feel a jerk from your Muppets that you haven't been expecting at all.

With her second, and then her third, drink, Lill—as usual—began to get rowdy. Her advances to Mr Achituko became more brazen than ever, and before long he downed his drink with uncharacteristic zeal and managed to get caught up in conversation by the bar. This gave Lill an opportunity to engage in raucous conversation with all the tables around her about the sexual prowess of 'darkies'. Even the Todmarshians got a mite embarrassed at this (though it was a subject they greatly enjoyed speculating on in hushed tones). Deborah thought her mother might conceivably take it as a reproof if she took herself off, so without a word she got up and went out.

Lill's reaction, however, was no different from her reaction to Fred's departure: she took care to say to Debbie's departing back: 'She's getting stuck up, that one. She's too proud for her own family.' Deborah, reaching the outside air and the darkness, leaned for a moment by the wall, laid her forehead against the coolness of it, and breathed deep. Then, with the resilience of youth, she shook herself and went off to play records with one of her friends.

Inside things were working up inexorably towards 'Lily the Pink'. Lill could sing other songs: her tastes tended towards the music-hall—to the blowsier numbers that she thought of as 'a bit of fun', where she could bring out all the innuendoes and add a few of her own. But 'Lily the Pink' was to her what 'My Way' is to Frank Sinatra: an irresistible mixture of Credo and blatant self-advertisement. She had been in her seventh heaven when the song was rediscovered. It beat 'Lily of Laguna' into a cocked hat. So now it came out on all feasts and high days, and the whole bar, after five or six hints, recognized its inevitability.

'All right,' said Lill at last, as if giving in to overwhelming popular demand. 'Stand back and give me a bit of room.' And pushing back the chairs in her vicinity she slipped off her apple green plasticated shoes and stood on the chintzy seats built solidly into the saloon bar wall. 'Come along, all,' she shrieked, 'help me with the chorus!'

And only half-reluctantly the bar turned in her direction, paid homage to the buxom bright figure standing there, bursting out of her electric blue dress and grinning encouragingly from under her outrageous mop of red hair.

'Go it, Lill,' someone said. 'We'll back you up.'

And as someone, from long training, began simulating the hurdy-gurdy accompaniment, Lill steadied herself on the bouncy cushions, opened up her healthy pink throat and let them have it.

'We'll drink-a-drink-a-drink to
Lily the Pink-the-Pink-the-Pink,
The saviour of the human ra-a-ace . . .'

She was in her element. This, she thought, should have been her life. Doing the Halls. Doing the Clubs up North. No class there, of course, but lots of life. She waved her hands for the chorus and a ragged sound emanated from the saloon bar regulars. 'Course everyone had life in them, Lill thought, but with some you had to work to get it out. She grinned encouragingly at them, and the sound grew louder and more in unison. She purred. She might have been God listening to the Hallelujah Chorus. She looked at little Mrs Watson, sitting with her back to her in the far corner. Funny: she hadn't had her back to her before. She looked at Mr Achituko over by the bar. Dear old Archie. What memories he'd take back with him to—wherever it was! Well, he can't say anyone was prejudiced here! Then her eyes rested on her boys, chairs pushed back, looking up at her smiling. That's what she liked—just her and the boys. That was how it should be. They were lovely boys. Good-looking too, though she said it herself and shouldn't.

And they adored her. You couldn't put it any other way. Look at them now—you could see it in their eyes. They simply adored her.

Gordon glanced at his watch surreptitiously as he raised his mug to drink. Twenty past. A bit of applause, a quenching of the thirst, and Lill would go. Half past on the dot on Saturday night. He'd join in the applause, then he'd make himself scarce. That should be easy enough. After one of Lill's performances everything became somehow more . . . flexible.

And indeed, when Lill bleated the song to its conclusion the bar, led by her sons, burst into proprietorial applause—she was *our* Lill, after all, and quite a character when all was said and done—and then the groups began loosening up, talking, laughing, and trotting to the bar for orders. And at the centre of it, as always, Lill, standing flushed and happy, accepting the compliments and finishing her drink.

'That's the stuff to give the troops,' she said. 'That Olivia Newton-John's got nothing on me, eh?'

Gordon, with an athlete's grace and quietness, sauntered through the various shifting and coalescing groups and out through the door marked 'Toilets'. The door led into a corridor with, at the far end, two doors marked with diagrams supposedly indicative of gender, which you had to peer at closely before pushing the one of your choice. But immediately to the left was a door leading out to the Rose and Crown's back yard, and close by it was a gate out to the street. Gordon was through it in a flash, and then walking coolly up the street towards home. No point in hurrying it. Might attract attention. Anyway, he only had to be sufficiently ahead of Lill for her not to recognize his back. His watch glowed phosphorescent in the darkness. Nine-twenty-eight. He was going to time this operation like a miler making an attempt on the record.

Back in the Rose and Crown Lill was collecting up her belongings—handbag, best coat, assorted make-up gear she had scattered over the table after a 'patching-up' operation. Once gathered together, she smiled her fearsome smile of maternal love at Brian.

'What you fancy for supper, love? Nice hamburger with a fried egg on it?'

'Lovely, Mum.'

'Where's Gordon?' Lill looked around the bar in the direction of Mrs Watson, and her eyes registered disappointment.

Brian swallowed. 'Gone for a leak, Mum.'

'Oh, you are common. Why can't you say "Gone to the toilet"?' Lill thought for a moment. 'Well, I suppose it being your birthday doesn't stop you having to go for a leak. I must be off. Tell him I'm doing hamburgers.'

'OK, Mum, I'll tell him.'

And Lill trolled through the Saloon Bar, gave a goodnight to practically everyone there, and pushed the door out into the street. Someone at the bar looked at his watch and said: 'Good old Lill. You could set your watch by her.'

Too right, thought Brian, draining his glass. Good old Lill.

The Saloon Bar settled down to be what in Lill's absence it always was: a dull little bar in a dull little town. They'll miss Lill when she's gone, thought Brian.

* * *

That night after hamburger (under-) and egg (over-cooked) Gordon and Brian undressed in their room and conversed in a whisper—unnecessarily, since nothing they said could have been heard over Fred's snores and Lill's noisy undressing in the next bedroom.

'I left at nine-twenty-seven,' hissed Gordon, 'and I was in position this end of Snoggers Alley at nine-thirty exactly. Actually I nipped into old mother Mitchell's garden in case she saw me, but in fact I'll stand under the telegraph post, where the lane widens out. Lill came by at nine-thirty-four, so I could have left a minute or two later, but I don't want to hurry—people might notice. And the four minutes' rest means I'll be in tip-top condition. Two minutes to do it, and I can be back in the Rose and Crown by nine-thirty-nine. Twelve minutes away in all. Plenty of people spend longer than that in the bog.'

'Old Fred in the mornings, for a start,' said Brian. They both giggled childishly, from nerves.

'Anyway, it won't matter if I'm a minute or two over time,' said Gordon. 'No one will notice I'm gone.'

Brian's face fell. 'Don't bank on it,' he said. 'Lill noticed, for a start.'

'What?' Gordon's voice suddenly assumed its normal baritone, and they both jumped nervously. But they needn't have bothered. Lill was in the bathroom, simultaneously cleaning her teeth and gargling her signature tune, and Fred was snoring away in the sleep of the just and stupid.

'What did she say?' hissed Gordon.

'She noticed you weren't there. When she went out. She asked where you were.'

'Oh Christ. Drawing the attention of everyone in the bar to the fact that I wasn't there.' Brian nodded. 'What did you say?'

'Well, I didn't say you were up in Snoggers timing an attempt to murder her this time next week . . .' They both sat on their beds, hunched forward in thought. 'What could I say? I said you'd gone to the bog.'

Gordon thought and thought, but came up with no very comforting solution. 'That's the trouble with Lill,' he said. 'You think she's absolutely predictable, then she springs a nasty surprise on you. We're going to have to think about this. If we're not careful we're going to be shopped, by Lill herself.'

CHAPTER 3

GINGERING THINGS UP

Sunday was a somnolent day at the Hodsdens'. It always was. Lill didn't like it, but she recognized there was nothing she could do against the collective lethargies of the other four. Saturday night was always Fred's big night of the week: darts at the Yachtsman's took it out of him, and Sundays he crept blearily about the house, all passions spent and considerably in overdraft. Brian and Gordon, as a rule, followed suit, if Gordon had nothing sporting on: they sprawled in armchairs reading the papers, they played cards or they watched television. 'It's natural,' Lill would explain to people, 'they work and play hard the rest of the week in their different ways—Gordon the physical, Brian more the—' she shied away from the word mental—'more the *psychological*!' Debbie just took herself off, quite inconspicuously. As usual, thought Lill bitterly, though she would certainly have gone on at her ceaselessly if she for once had been around.

So Sunday they slept, ate well of Gordon's birthday dinner of beef, Yorkshire pudding and three veg, followed by tinned peaches, then reread the *Sunday Mirror* and the *Express* and watched Bruce Forsyth on the enormous colour television that Lill said (and Fred believed her) she had picked up for practically nothing from a family going to live abroad. The chocolates, which they opened after tea, turned out to be all soft centres, which Gordon did not like. Still, Lill did, and the evening was punctuated by the sound of Lill's pudgy hand reaching down into the box and scuffling around in the paper that crackled like money.

'Come on, Gordon,' she would say, 'tuck in. They cost the earth.'

'I've had enough for the moment, Mum.'

' "He has a proud stomach, that boy",' murmured Brian.

'There's nothing wrong with his stomach,' protested Lill. 'He's got a lovely body. Not an ounce of surplus anywhere.' And she leered at her eldest and reached down again into the chocolate box.

But the consequence was that Monday morning Lill felt in need of some sort of reviver, a tonic, something to put pep back into the system and get zing coursing through her veins. Which meant, though she was largely unconscious of this herself, that she was in need of a good stand-up row. All her best rows occurred on Mondays, as all the family but herself realized—it was a day that might well have been observed by family, neighbours and circle of acquaintance as a day of lamentation, fasting, and general breast-beating.

At breakfast Lill was in high good humour, and, quite unaware that she was working up to a row or two, she planned them. She scrambled some eggs to a leathery consistency and then found she'd forgotten the salt. She toasted the thin sliced loaf into wavy North Sea shapes and slapped them in a pile down on the kitchen table.

'Eat it while it's warm,' she said.

'Here, Mum,' said Gordon, poking a spoon sceptically at the marmalade dish, 'what's this?'

'Mother's special,' replied Lill cheerily. 'Had a lot of jam jars with just a bit left in them, and I put 'em all together. I think I'll patent the idea. Call it plumberry marmalade or something.'

Gordon groaned.

'Tasty!' said Fred, chewing meditatively.

When Brian and Debbie had run off at the last minute to catch the bus to school, and when Gordon and Fred had cycled off in opposite directions to work (Christ, thought Lill to herself, we must be the only family in the whole bloody town without a car. Just my luck), Lill washed up and made the beds—all but Debbie's, because a girl of that age ought to make her own—and while she did it she meditated ways of giving a lift to the day, gingering things up in her vicinity, giving life a spot of zip. So round about half past ten, when she knew she'd be having coffee, she stuffed a fag in her mouth and went in next door to see her mother.

'Do you want a cup?' her mother asked, having that moment sat down with hers at the kitchen table.

'Just to be friendly,' said Lill. 'Make it milky.' Her mother, without a word, got up and put a saucepan of milk on the gas-ring.

About the only thing Lill had inherited from her mother had been her regularity—that was how she knew she'd be settling down to a quiet cup at half past ten. In other ways they were as different as camembert and gorgonzola. Old Mrs Casey, widow long since of a plumber in a small way, was short, fat and formidable more from her grim silence than her tongue. Wherever she went she was a Presence, steel-eyed, incorruptible, disapproving. She had her Standards, unspoken, unwritten, unanswerable, and she was openly contemptuous of anyone who wittingly or unwittingly sinned against them. She cut no figure in Todmarsh at large but she attended Methodist Chapel morning and evening, rain or shine, of a Sunday. In fact, the image of nonconformity she presented was of so rigid and regrettable a kind that one trendy minister had offered to bring the service to her if she would only stay home. She had stared him out of countenance, and finally said: 'I'm not gone that soft yet.' In all her life she had had only one failure, and made only one mistake. The failure was Lill, the mistake was consenting to come and live next door to her.

'I've been thinking,' said Lill, starting straight in.

'Oh yes . . . ?' Grimly, very grimly.

'About Debbie moving in here with you . . .'

Mrs Casey removed the milk from the ring and poured it with rock-steady hand into the cup which had been a wedding present back in the days when a tea-service was a possession for life.

'As far as I'm concerned there's never been any question of it,' she said. 'The question doesn't arise. And don't drop cigarette ash in your cup, for goodness sake. Milk costs the earth these days.'

But such diversionary tactics had less than no chance of success. Why had Lill put a cigarette in other than to annoy her mother, who hated above all to see her with it hanging loosely from her mouth?

'That's where you're so daft, Mum,' said Lill, deftly

aiming ash in the direction of the stove. 'You're not as young as you were. You need someone here all the time, to see you're all right.'

'Hmm,' said Mrs Casey, settling down into her chair again and taking up her coffee cup, 'you needn't pretend it's concern for me that's behind it.'

'Well, there's Gordon and Bri too, of course. They need a bedroom to themselves each. Stands to reason at their age. Debbie's would just suit Bri down to the ground. Give him room for all them books of his.'

'Not to mention the fact that you'd be pleased to get Debbie out of your hair. Well, I've told you before, it's not on. I'm too old to go looking after a girl of her age. My notions are not her notions, and it's silly to pretend she'd put up with it. After the sort of life she's had in your house. I'm seventy-five. That's no time of life to start bringing up a teenager.'

'It's because you're so bloody old you need somebody here,' said Lill, sucking in her coffee noisily. 'Someone around all the time to see that you're still living and breathing.'

This appeal to the perennial fear of the old cut no ice with Mrs Casey. 'It's not me has to be afraid of dying. I'm ready. And it's not as though I'm *alone*, with all you lot living next door. The boys are very good. They pop in.'

Lill's voice took on a harsh edge: 'I'm not having my boys running in and out here every five minutes to see if you're stretched out. They've got better things to do. You've gotter have your fun while you're young.'

'Of course,' said Mrs Casey cunningly, 'if you want

the boys to have a room of their own, then Gordon could move in here with me.'

''Ere, you're not having my Gordon! What a cheek! That's disgusting, an old woman like you!'

'He's older,' continued Mrs Casey, paying no attention, 'so there wouldn't be the same problems. He could go his own way. And it's always easier with a boy, as you know.'

The conversation had taken a turn that Lill Hodsden had not at all anticipated, and she tried to change tack. 'The boys are staying together, and that's flat. You only suggested it because you knew they wouldn't—'

'I knew *you* wouldn't have it, more like.'

'You're just a selfish old woman. You haven't changed a bit all the years I've known you. Think about nothing but yourself. All my childhood you kept me down, stopped me having my bit of fun—'

Mrs Casey sniffed expressively. 'I tried to stop you leading a life of sin and depravity—'

'No need to chuck the ruddy Bible at me. Nobody gives a damn about that sort of thing these days. You were jealous, that was all, under all that religious talk. Jealous. That's why you forced me to marry Fred—'

'Forced you! Ha!' Mrs Casey let out a bitter, reminiscent laugh. 'You'd have married Jack the Ripper only to get away from home. When you went off and married Fred I was just pleased it was no worse.'

'How would you know how worse it was? You know nothing about it. You never understood me. You've made trouble in the family all the time you've been here. You've never fitted in—I should never have let you come here.'

'Went down on your bended knees,' amended Mrs Casey, who never let swervings from the literal truth pass uncorrected. 'So you'd have a home help and someone to dump the kids on to when it suited you.'

'And a fat lot of dumping I've been able to do on you!' said Lill bitterly.

Mrs Casey smiled a hard, complacent smile. 'Not much, I grant you. I wasn't having any of that. Why should I? I'm not so green as I'm cabbage-looking. You met your match wi' me, Lill. You and I'll never get on, because you're not as smart as you think you are, and I'm a deal smarter!'

Stung perhaps by the truth of it, Lill clattered her coffee cup back on the saucer and stood up. But before she could frame a sufficiently annihilating parting shot, her mother said:

'Perhaps that's the trouble with Debbie, too, eh? She's a mite smarter than you already.'

Lill banged out the back door, barged past the milkman, who had been idly listening, and bounced through the back garden home. Mrs Casey went about her morning dusting and sweeping with a sprightliness she hadn't felt in her when she got up.

It had given a bit of excitement, thought Lill, but still, it wasn't much of a row. Which meant, of course, that its outcome was not at all the one she had been banking on. It certainly hadn't given the day the central focus she had unconsciously planned for it. Every day, for Lill, had to have some kind of focal point she could remember as she lay in bed—some moment when she stood in the spotlight in one or other kind of triumph. Through the rest of the morning, and over dinner with Fred and Gordon—shepherd's pie and tinned pears and cream, rushed and scamped as always—she wondered how to give it that focus. When she had washed up she seemed to make a quick decision: she emptied the contents of the sugar bowl back into the packet, and she cantered up the road to little Mrs Watson.

'Coo-ee,' she shouted at the door, which stood open: 'anyone at home?'

Mrs Watson flinched, being just around the door trying to get her stove to light. But then, she flinched automatically at Lill. Todmarsh was a small town, though, and open warfares were best avoided, so she hid her dislike and irritation behind a brave social face and said: 'Hello, Mrs Hodsden.'

'Oh he*llo*,' said Lill, steaming in and assuming a dreadfully refined manner, like a parody of one of the more uppitty Archers. 'I didn't see you round there. *Could* you help me? I clean forgot sugar down the shops today. *Could* you lend me a spot, save me going down before tomorrow?'

'Of course,' said Ann Watson. She refrained from wondering why Lill had not gone borrowing at any of the nine or ten houses that separated them in Windsor Avenue. She merely took the bowl and went to the kitchen cupboard, her thick, long hair shielding her face from Lill's hungry gaze. But when she brought it back and handed it over she could not avoid looking at her and paying the social price of a polite smile. She received in return a smile of combined sympathy and good cheer that oozed over her and dripped down, as if she'd been crowned with a plate of cold porridge.

'I *was* pleased to see you out on Saturday night,'

said Lill, her voice throbbing with personal concern. 'I thought to myself: "She's coming round," I
thought.'

'I beg your pardon?' said Ann Watson, sheet ice
in her voice.

'Getting over it,' pursued Lill, blithely unconscious.
'Coming back to life, and getting about a bit again.
Because it doesn't do, you know.'

'What doesn't?' said Ann unwisely, still frozen
hard.

'Giving yourself up to grief,' said Lill luxuriantly.

But for once Lill had hit the nail on the head.
Ann Watson had been married less than two years
when her husband had been shot in the back while
on patrol in Northern Ireland. He had died the next
day and become two lines in the national newspapers.
The War Office had flown her to his funeral. Her
life, it seemed to her, was like a snapped twig, and
she was living the broken end now. It is not fashionable to talk of being grief-stricken, any more than
it is fashionable to talk of happy marriages, but Ann
Watson had been grief-stricken because her marriage
had been happy. And she didn't fool herself that
happy marriages happen twice. Even now, more than
two years later, all the social gestures seemed difficult and meaningless—even the social gesture of looking after her little girl. She constructed a daily round,
and followed it like a somnambulant nun. At moments
of stress she had visions of her husband falling in the
street, and the pointlessness of it, the futility, en-
raged her to the breaking point. Hardest to bear was
the feeling that people she met could not face her pain,
tried to butter it over with clichés. Time was not, she
had found, the great healer.

'I've been back teaching part-time for eighteen months,' she said. 'It doesn't exactly look as if I'd given myself up to grief.' As she said it she kicked herself: why should she justify herself to this woman? Someone she didn't even like?

'Oh, *that's* not what I meant,' said Lill, happily unconscious of opposition or offence. 'I meant going out and enjoying yourself, getting a kick out of life again. That's what I want to see.'

'It's none of your business,' said Ann, back to the stove and feeling pressed into a corner by her ignorant goodwill.

' 'Course it's our business. We've all been concerned about you, everyone along the road. It's just that old Lill's the only one to speak out honest about it. It's not nice to see someone moping for so long. I know my Gordon's been very concerned.'

'I'm sure it's kindly meant,' said Ann, aware that Lill was pushing her into the stalest of conversational clichés, and fearful that she would soon be reduced to the purest fishwife abuse. 'I just wish you all wouldn't bother.'

'He's a very kind-hearted chap, my Gordon. He feels things, know what I mean? 'Course, he was in the army like your hubby—five years he was in. Did his bit in Northern Ireland too, like they all have to. I expect him and your chap are very alike, really.'

'They're nothing like,' said Ann shortly.

'Oh, I don't mean in the face, or anything, just in their natures. Though I will say this, though I shouldn't as his mum, but you wouldn't find a better-looking, better setup chap than my Gordon.' The voice became more insistent. *'Would you?'*

'I really can't say I've thought about it.'

'Go on. Don't tell me. You've thought about it all right. I know what it's like when you're young. What are you? Twenty-four? Twenty-five?' Lill's leer split her face in two, a great cracked doll's face, surmounted by a shrieking red mop. 'I know what it's like being twenty-five, widow or no widow. Now, your David was a nice-looking chap, I'm sure, and one in a million, but he wasn't the only fish in the sea and why should you pretend he was? He's been gone two years and more now. And there's things that a girl like you needs at your age—'

'Do you mind—?'

'And there's my Gordon, he's really got an eye for you. You'd go lovely together, I know it. I can just see you, together. You might be made for each other. Go on—admit it: you wouldn't say no to a bit of you-know-what now and again, would you? No girl ought to be ashamed of that. Wouldn't my Gordon just suit you down to the ground, eh?'

Ann Watson faced her across the kitchen table, and Lill's evil old face suddenly touched a nerve which made her control snap as it never had since the day her husband had died: 'You disgusting old bag,' she shrieked, red in the face. 'You're pimping for your own son.'

'Words!' said Lill, momentarily disconcerted and retreating towards the door, clutching her sugar bowl. 'I wouldn't have expected words like that from a girl of your education. That's what comes of trying to do a bit of good in the world. I only wanted to help you, because I saw you needed it. All I want's for you both to be comfortable.'

'Get out of my house, you old harridan,' yelled Ann, and as Lill turned tail and started down the step she marched over and slammed the door brutally on her retreating ankle. Then she tottered over to the kitchen table and sat down, clutching the legs of it until her knuckles were white, racked by violent, silent sobs that would not come out in tears.

Limping down the road, having enjoyed herself hugely, Lill nevertheless thought to herself: I don't think she'd do for my Gordon, after all. He'd never want to get hitched to a girl with a temper like that.

CHAPTER 4

A BIT ON THE SIDE

Lill Hodsden's colour television—a large, poor-quality model, out of which salmon-pink announcers gaped at her as from a fish-bowl, dressed in shiny turquoise suits unbecoming their age and dignity—was in fact a present from a friend, though for form's sake, and because she liked lying when it could give her a delicious sense of romantic intrigue, she had invented the family emigrating to foreign parts. It was a present she had been grateful for at the time ('Oh, it's *ever* so much prettier,' she had said, and indeed she had sat for hour after hour gazing at washy-blue hills alive with the sound of music), but the first fine bloom of gratitude had by now worn off, hardly at all prolonged by the occasional gift of cash. She was beginning to wonder whether the time wasn't ripe for another more substantial tribute. She'd have to start hinting, very delicately, to Mr Corby.

It was a Corby evening tonight, Monday. Lill always gave her boys—and inevitably her family—a cooked tea. She prided herself on it. When Brian and Debbie had got back from school by bus about five, and when Gordon and Fred had separately cycled home from work, she served them all toasted cheese and Beefomite, an invention of her own she was very proud of, though *Woman's Home* had surprisingly failed to print the recipe when she submitted it for their Tastisnax page. Debbie ate only one little triangle, then went out and got a lump of cheese from the 'fridge and ostentatiously nibbled it, heedless of Lill's cold, hard stares. The rest of them had got used to it, and managed to get it down.

'Champion,' said Fred, licking his lips.

By seven-fifteen Lill had smoked two fags cadged from Gordon, washed up the tea things ('By rights I ought to have a machine, with a family this size') and listned to *The Archers* ('That Shula's a right little madam, just like my Debbie'). At twenty past seven she took down her leopard-skin coat from the hook in the hall, fixed a perky green hat on her scarlet mop, and poked her head round the front-room door:

'I'm just going round to sit with Mrs Corby for an hour or two,' she called.

'Right you are,' said Fred, breaking out of a doze.

Debbie was upstairs in the much-discussed bedroom, Brian was in the back room doing a history essay for the morning on Benthamism and nineteenth-century industrial legislation, and Gordon was upstairs changing into his track suit preparatory to going jogging. To all of them Lill shrilled blithelȳ 'Won't be gone long!', and then clip-clopped out into Windsor Avenue with a silly complacent smile on her face which gave her away to the merest cat, sunning itself on the garden wall.

Mrs Corby was an invalid who for five years now had kept to her room, laid low by an indefinable illness that doctors in the last century would probably have labelled 'nervous prostration'. Now and again in summer her husband, with the help of a neighbour, bundled her into the car, wrapped up like an oversized and querulous baby, and took her for a drive to Portsea along the coast, or inland to some of the beauty spots and picturesque villages of South-West England, at all of which Mrs Corby glared malevolently, as if this was what she was glad to have got away from. This was her only contact with civilization at large. She had a nature ill-adapted to friendship, being a thoroughly nasty woman with a vinegar-soaked tongue and a need to cut everybody within sight down to half her own size, so she had no visitors. She saw her husband, the doctor, and the twice-weekly char. She had never in her life, certainly, spoken to Lill Hodsden, for in Todmarsh, as elsewhere, there were circles within circles, and Drusilla Corby was on the inner, and Lill Hodsden the outer line. By now this was irrelevant. For Lill she was just an excuse, a convenience, a lie that could not be checked up on. W. Hamilton Corby had once described her to Lill as a legal fiction, and Lill, thinking he'd said friction, had snarled: 'Christ, she's that all right.'

She let herself into the large, weather-mellowed, red-brick house, with the feeble pretence of battlements and turret windows, and went straight through the hall to the study at the back. Finding nobody there, she opened the bar-cupboard in the far corner (rosewood lined with pink silk—Corby had had it made specially) and mixed herself a gin and tonic. Holding her glass in a sophisticated manner, imagining herself to be Princess Grace at a diplomatic reception in Monaco, she went over to the desk and casually went through the correspondence there. Then she remembered to take off her parody leopard-skin, threw it over the desk chair, and settled herself on the leather-covered sofa, fingering it meditatively and pricing it in her mind. It wouldn't have been *her* choice, but the cost of it excited her. When finally Hamilton Corby came into the room, muttering 'She's a bit troublesome tonight,' Lill drained her glass, waited till he had safely closed the door, then cackled and said: 'When isn't she?'

W. Hamilton Corby (born Wilf Corby, he had taken in his wife's surname when she had made him the happiest in Todmarsh, and one of the wealthier) was not a romantic figure, looked at objectively. The impression one took away was of sagging tummy, baggy trousers, and watery, shifty eyes. He was the sort of man one sees in droves at the better sort of main-road pubs, boasting about their deals by the bar with their sagging, baggy, shifty fellows, or sitting silent at tables with their wives. No, beyond his income he scored few points as a lover, and more often than not all he wanted on Lill's visits was a befuddled fumble. More's the pity, as Lill often said to herself.

'She's a poor creature,' said Corby, settling himself on the sofa and putting his hand absent-mindedly on Lill's knee, apparently because it was there. He went through, as if by rote, the litany of phrases he always used about his wife. 'She's her own worst enemy. She makes no one unhappy but herself. I don't know what she'd do without me. Because I can tell you this: she'd never get anyone else to stop with her, pay them what she might. She's the sort nobody can help because she won't help herself.'

Lill sat complacently through this, the terms of which were as well known to her as a weather forecast. When he came to a stop the hand went further up her thigh. Lill would have liked another gin and tonic, but she thought he might as well do whatever he wanted to do or was capable of doing, and then they could be comfy. Five minutes later she got her gin.

'Business booming?' she asked, sipping. It was one of her four conversational openings.

Hamilton Corby grunted. 'Not bad. Could be worse. Thank God we're a small firm, making small boats people can still afford. If we'd built liners or tankers we'd have been in the hands of the receiver long ago. Or taken over by Wedgie Benn.'

'How's my Gordon doing? All right?'

Corby grunted again. 'All right. He's a good worker. Not that there's much for him to do. I only took him on to oblige, as you know. But he pulls his weight . . . Shouldn't have thought it was really his line, though.'

Lill preened herself and put on her Lady Muck face. 'Well, of *course* he should really be doing something *far* better, something with *lots* more class. He's a boy with *tremendous* potential.' She relaxed a little, and immediately collapsed into bathos: 'I've always thought my Gordon ought to be in films.'

Hamilton Corby said nothing. The last time he'd been to the cinema had been in the Anna Neagle-Michael Wilding era. Gordon didn't remind him all that much of Michael Wilding.

'He's got the looks,' continued Lill, looking dreamily ahead over her glass of gin. 'That nobody could deny. A real smasher. And he's got something else . . . A sort of dangerous quality.'

Corby did not consider that last statement as

seriously as he might. 'Can he act?' he asked nastily.

'He used to do marvellous imitations as a child,' rejoined Lill, unperturbed. 'Killing he was, had us all in stitches. They're both very talented, my boys.'

'He strikes me more as the sporty type,' said Corby, who genuinely liked Gordon. 'Should have gone to college, become a P.E. teacher or something.'

'Well, of course that's what I *wanted,*' said Lill, hearing the notion for the first time. 'It would have suited him down to the ground. But no, it had to be the army. He *would* go. Christ, when I think of that Mrs Watson's hubby, dead at twenty-four, I get the cold shivers. Thank God my Gordon got out.' She suddenly thought of something and cackled. 'They both got out in a way, eh?'

She quietened down after a bit, when Hamilton Corby merely contemplated his whisky glass mournfully. 'Oh dear, aren't I awful? Anyway, as I was saying, Gordon's *not* really got as far as he ought to have done. That's why I want him to have a car.'

The remarkable logical leap from vocational heights to physical distances did not escape Hamilton Corby. He declined to leap at once in the required direction. He said: 'Plenty of cars around.'

'Of course, I meant a sort of family car,' said Lill. 'Only Gordon could drive it. Brian too when he's a bit older, because there's nothing unmechanical about him, for all his brains . . .' She paused for a little, and then added meaningfully: 'You've got more money than you know what to do with.'

'*Nobody's* got more money than they know what to do with,' replied Corby, with intense conviction.

'Oh, go on. You wouldn't even notice a sum like that,' said Lill, nudging him encouragingly. Hamilton Corby was not stupid: he may have got where he was (and paid for it) by marriage, but he had kept there by a modicum of sharpness. He had several ways of not getting caught by the likes of Lill.

'My brother-in-law's got an old Mini,' he said eventually; 'belongs to his wife, but she never uses it. He's thinking of selling it.'

'That wasn't the kind of car I was thinking about,' said Lill.

'I'm sure it wasn't.' And Hamilton Corby smiled a sly, aqueous smile and held his peace. Lill thought she'd let the subject drop for a moment, and the two turned to other things.

'Hey, I had the chance of a lifetime last week,' she said eventually, as the hands of the clock neared nine-thirty. Her fat, coarse face had brightened at the very thought.

'What was that?'

'Guy Fawcett next door. Made what you might call an indecent suggestion.'

'Oh? What was that?'

'What do you mean what was that? What do you think it was? Wanted to go to bed with me, that's what. He's often home during the day, and his wife's out at work. And of course, none of my lot's home during the day.'

'What did you say?'

'Called him a dirty old man and said he ought to be ashamed. Doesn't do to jump at it first time.' She cast a sideways glance at Hamilton Corby, sagging apathetically on the sofa beside her, and said: 'Not that he is old, not by a long chalk. About forty-five, I'd say. Not much older than me . . . Got a good job, too . . . He's a car salesman.'

'Perhaps you'd better go to him for your car,' said Corby, with unexpected quickness of mind. As a ploy for arousing jealousy, Guy Fawcett's indecent proposal seemed less than a total success. She began collecting herself together.

'Of course, he's a very attractive man,' she said, persistent. 'Tremendous shoulders. And what I'd call a really sensitive face. You never know when you'll get that sort of proposition again . . .' She shook her head meaningfully.

'See you Thursday, Lill?'

'Shouldn't wonder. Same time.' At the study door she gave him a tremendous passionate kiss five seconds long, and after tiptoeing through the hall another at the front door.

'Don't you worry about Fawcett,' she whispered, as if he had; 'I can put him in his place any time.'

'Don't take any nonsense from him, Lill,' said Corby, playing along.

'Not more than I want to. Keep your pecker up. It can't last for ever, you know. If she was gone, I'd marry you like a shot.'

Hamilton Corby, who knew he could do very much better if marriage were in question, said: 'What about Fred?'

'Oh, I'd soon get rid of *Fred*,' returned Lill, her whisper more urgent. 'Never you mind how. Ta-ta for now.'

Above them on the first floor a door closed. On the step, taking a last genteel peck, they heard nothing. Then Lill set off at her usual brisk pace down Balaclava Road and turned into the enveloping shadows of Snoggers Alley. She was not altogether satisfied with her evening, but still, a seed had been planted.

And if the worst came to the worst, a Mini would be better than nothing. So when she got home, at nine-forty prompt, she was quite her normal cheery self.

'That's my good turn for the day done!'

'How was she?' asked Fred, who was in the same half-asleep state he had been in when she went out, this time in front of a TV Western.

Lill shook her head gloomily. 'It's a terrible disease. She's in purgery the whole time. The doctors can't even put a name to it.'

Fred nodded. He never showed any greater curiosity than this about her twice-weekly visits. His store of curiosity was tiny at the best of times. The rest of the family, sprawled around the television in various attitudes of inattention, kept tactfully silent.

'Do you know,' said Lill, who could never keep quiet about anything that was on her mind. 'I think it's time we bought a car.' Gordon looked at Brian and Brian looked at Gordon, but neither of them said anything. Debbie sniffed and left the room. 'We'd've had one years ago if it hadn't been for buying Gordon out of the army. I think I know where we could pick one up dirt cheap. I've always said, it's what you boys need. Get you out so's you can have a good time. Meet a few girls.'

'I thought I was supposed to be marked down for Mrs Watson,' said Gordon. 'I don't need a car to go courting her—she just lives up the road.'

'Mrs Watson! That stuck-up little tailor's dummy! Christ! Whatever gave you that idea? You're a sight too good to take up with other men's leavings.'

Lill always let her family know when she changed her mind.

* * *

'She's screwing a car out of him now,' said Gordon to Brian, when at last they had escaped from rusks and Ovalmix and had reached the womblike safety of their bedroom. 'God, what a cheek she's got!'

'Would you have the nerve to drive round in a car that was the price of your mother's shame?' demanded Brian with a melodramatic gesture of the arms.

'Frankly, I wouldn't give it a second thought. Only I don't think I'll be getting the chance. Lill's next ride is going to be in the back of a hearse.'

Brian shivered when it was put that bluntly. 'Funny to think about it. Free, after all these years of . . . of being her doormats. I wish I felt better.'

Gordon looked at him keenly. 'What do you mean, better? What's the matter?'

'Just this ruddy cough. It's the climate. "Bronchial isle, all isles excelling", as the poet said. They shouldn't have put people down in this climate.'

'It's not the climate does things to you. It's Lill. It's just some nervous thing. Remember last year—you weren't any better in Tunisia.'

Brian, lying on his bed with an unread book, shifted uneasily at the mention of Tunisia, as he always did. 'Christ, no wonder I didn't feel up to much,' he muttered. 'What with Lill and all. Remember Lill on the plane?'

The two heads on their pillows—Gordon's dark and purposeful, Brian's fair and distressed—lay for a moment in silence as last year's holiday in Tunisia came back to them. It had been explained to Lill that the firm they were travelling with was 'up market', and, when she expressed bewilderment, the term had been spelled out in words of one syllable. But she never quite understood that the people on this trip

were a different sort from the mob they had been
with to Benidorm three years before. Just in those
early moments, when everyone was settling into their
seats, swapping with each other at most a murmured
comment on the rate of exchange or the price of Glen-
fiddich, Lill showed she misjudged the prevailing
mood by shrieking across the plane to Gordon, six
rows in front: 'Soon be there now, Gord! How long
will it be, d'you think, before some sheikh snatches
me up in his passionate arms and takes me off to his
harem, eh?' And as soon as the 'Fasten Seat Belts'
sign was switched off she was swaying along the aisle
to the loo singing 'The Sheikh of Arabee-ee' with
special smiles at all the more desirably distinguished
men on the trip. One frozen air hostess at the back of
the plane raised a plucked eyebrow at the other
frozen air hostess at the front; the up-market travellers
glanced sideways at each other and coughed in the
backs of their throats. Still over the Channel, and
everyone had got Lill's number. None of them exchanged a word with Lill for the rest of the fort-
night. 'They're a stuffy lot,' Lill kept saying. 'I prefer
the wogs. Don't understand what they're going on
about, but at least they're friendly.'

At last Brian, deep in memories, said: 'No it's not
the climate. It's Lill.'

'And it's Lill,' said Gordon, 'makes us the laughing-stocks of the town. Disgraces us every time we try
to climb out of the mud. You know what people say
about you and me?'

'Yes,' said Brian. 'I know. Still, when all's said and
done—'

'Anyway,' said Gordon quickly, 'your role is to be

my alibi. Your health doesn't mater. You haven't got to do anything.'

'It sounds a bit feeble,' complained Brian.

'What's the point of all this training I do if I can't even kill off my own mother? It's got to be one of us, not both, and obviously I'm the fit one.' He stubbed out his cigarette in the ashtray. 'I'm even giving up smoking tomorrow—for the duration. Yours is the brainy bit. You've got to convince the police I was in the pub the whole evening, except for the odd minute in the bog. You've got to have it off pat, the whole story.'

'What about if Lill opens her big mouth and draws attention to it, like she did on Saturday?'

'We've got to make damn sure she doesn't.' Gordon lay on his back, looking darkly at the ceiling. 'I've been thinking about it. I think we could work it like this: if I slip off a couple of minutes before Lill's due to go, and say "I'm just nipping over to have a word with John" or Chris or whoever happens to be in the pub that night—"see you at supper", then she won't comment on my not being there. And I'll make sure I do have a word with them some time in the evening, in case anyone asks. Either just before or just after.'

'You've got to be careful just after,' said Brian. 'I've read about the physical effects of murdering someone. It makes you want to—'

'I know it makes you want to—well, that's what Lill's done to me all her life.'

'Just be careful. Even if you're only a bit jittery, people notice things. You'd better just come back to the table and talk to me . . . What are you going to do it with? Not your hands?'

'No,' said Gordon. 'Though I could. But it's too risky. I'll use rope. I can get a short bit from work.'

'They'd be able to trace the type.'

'It's common stuff. You can buy it anywhere.'

'Why not just hit her on the head?'

'It might not kill her, not with that thick skull. If I hit her several times, there'd probably be blood. That's one thing I can't risk, blood . . . Anyway,' he added slowly, 'I don't think it would give me the same pleasure.' A smile was on his full lips.

'You're really looking forward to this, aren't you?'

'Yeah, baby brother, I'm looking forward to it.' He looked mockingly at Brian across the bare length of their room. 'Aren't you? Touch of the cold feet?'

'No,' said Brian carefully. 'No. But if I was actual-ly *doing* it . . . The alibi business, that's a piece of cake. I'll enjoy that. The other, the . . . strangling, I don't know if I could. She's our mother.' He swal-lowed. 'When it comes down to it, I don't suppose she's meant any harm.'

'Christ, you bloody intellectuals,' hissed Gordon through his teeth. 'You never go straight at a thing, do you? Never meant any harm? What else has she ever meant? In twenty years you'll be toasting her on the anniversary of all this with tears in your eyes: "To the finest Mum a man ever had!" '

'Don't be daft . . .'

'And in twenty years, I'll join you.'

CHAPTER 5

TUESDAY

Lill's life changed course somewhat on Tuesday, though by no means as drastically as it was to later in the week. The day began in the usual way, with the family crawling reluctantly out of their beds, quarrelling over the bathroom and loo, slouching down to breakfast half asleep (a good job, really, because the poached eggs were hard as stones), and gradually dispersing themselves in their various directions. Once that was over, the day opened up with manifold possibilities for Lill. Now she could dispose of her hours as she would, captain of her fate, mistress of her soul; meaning, in fact, that she could plan any manner of mischief she set her heart on.

Lill wondered whether Guy Fawcett would be home next door during the day.

The thought stayed with her as she performed in her slapdash way her various early morning chores. The cat—black with white paws and whiskers, and knowing eyes that saw through Lill all right—demanded breakfast, and Lill reached down a tin. As she opened it she noticed a By Appointment sign on the label, and said to herself: Blimey, you'd have thought she could afford something better than this! She washed up the breakfast things, and slapped a greasy

cloth over the kitchen table. Then she put some coke
on the kitchen stove and emptied the ashes from underneath. Throughout she kept half an eye on the
kitchen window and the gardens outside.

At nine-fifteen Guy Fawcett appeared beyond the
next-door fence, large and visible, and carrying a
spade which he showed no inclination to use.

Didn't do to seem too eager. Lill knew the moves
in the game as well as anyone alive. She went upstairs to make the beds, opened the bedroom windows
wide, and carolled in her crow-scaring singing voice
the first two lines or so of 'Oh, What a Beautiful
Morning', over and over. She knew the ropes. It gave
him an opening. 'You sound happy today,' he could
say when she finally emerged into the back garden.
As she made Brian and Gordon's beds her eyes strayed
to the figure of Guy Fawcett, wandering around his
back lawn in the pallid April sunshine. His heart
doesn't seem to be in it, she thought. Better give him
something to keep his pecker up. So when she went
downstairs, she took out the sink-tidy, with the rubbish from breakfast, and slapped the contents into
the dust-bin, humming cheerily the while a healthy
Cliff Richard number.

'You sound happy this fine morning,' said Guy Fawcett from over the garden fence. 'Come into a fortune?'

'That's right,' said Lill, not pausing in her trot back
to the kitchen. 'I come into the pools. Just like that
woman said, it's going to be "Spend, Spend, Spend"
with me.'

'It would be too with you, Lill,' said Fawcett, his
bass baritone throbbing with admiration. Lill laughed
all the way down the scale, threw him a sideways look

that could mean whatever he chose it to, and charged through the back door. The first move had been made. The gunfighters were circling warily round the dusty town square, waiting for the moment when they would come out into the open, all cylinders blazing.

Lill hurried through the rest of her chores. After all, though it doesn't do to seem too anxious, still— Fred and Gordon would be back at five past one. Another little bout of teasing would be strictly within the rules of the game, but it would take time. She finished her scanty Hoovering, decided not to dust the bits of brass, china dogs, cheap African pots and other ornaments dotted around her mantelpiece and window ledges, then fetched her handbag and put on a bit of make-up lovingly in front of the mirror: not too much—didn't want to make it too obvious; not too little—have to give him an excuse for mentioning it. She smirked at herself when she had finished: she could still show the young 'uns a thing or two! This done, she armed herself with a fearsome pair of secateurs from Fred's gardening drawer, and sallied out into the fresh air.

The garden was Fred's responsibility. When not tending the parish parks he came back to dig his own potato patch, and it would never have occurred to him to complain at this. Now and then Lill acted in a supervisory capacity, told him what she wanted, where, and so on; but basically she took no interest in it. Flowers, like cats, were too involved in their own intricate magnificence to minister to her self-love. So beyond demanding great clumps of gladioli, peonies, or any other slightly monstrous bloom that caught her eye in other gardens, she left it to Fred. And it looked like it. Fred had his successes, mainly turnips and chrysanthemums, but he could not be said to run to a green finger. The Hodsdens' back garden was a dull little patch of earth.

Still, spring flowers there were, and the odd bush she could make feints at, in pretence of pruning. Which is more than could be said for Guy Fawcett's garden, which was a weedy lawn, and beyond that a wilderness: tall straggly bits of weeds, grasses and flowers that had been planted and forgotten. Any less blatant person would have been embarrassed at the pretence of ever working in it or caring what happened to it.

'Hot work this,' said Guy, unbending from doing nothing very much by a border and drawing a fleshy arm across his brow.

'Got to be done,' said Lill, flashing a head-on smile while snapping away at a depressed and dusty rose-bush that looked more in need of pep-pills than pruning. 'You don't get anything in this world you don't work for.'

'True,' said Guy, though neither of them believed a word of it: neither of them had got where they were, or enjoyed the pleasures they did enjoy, as a result of the sweat of their brows. Guy weighed straight in, as was his custom. 'God, you look a million dollars today, Lill. I don't know how you do it. Time doesn't just stand still with you. It walks backwards, like leaving the Queen's presence.'

This flowery compliment was typical of Guy in the early stages, but it was wasted on Lill, who knew nothing of the mysteries of locomotion before royalty. 'Go on,' she said, which was a good all-purpose remark she made a lot of use of. 'Few more years and I'll be past my prime!'

'I shan't live to see that,' returned Guy. As though drawn by invisible plastic gardening twine they both approached the waist-high fence. Lill threw up her arms in a gesture of girlish ecstasy and exclaimed. 'Oh, I love Spring!'

They looked at the scratchy earth, poked through by the dusty leaves of newly-sprouting bulbs and sighed sentimentally. 'Yes, it makes you think, Spring,' said Guy. His thick, sensual self-admiring lips slid into a meaningful grin: 'Eh Lill? Doesn't Spring make you think of a lot of things you could be doing?'

'Maybe,' said Lill. 'And I don't suppose you mean digging the potato patch either.'

'Not exactly,' agreed Guy, the grin still fixed but mobile on his lips, and his eyes resting on her powdery face. 'But when you get to our age—say thirty-five—'

'Say twenty-five if you like,' said Lill agreeably.

'—you realize there's some things—things you want to do—and that time's not on your side any longer—that you'd be silly *not* to do them if that's what you fancy—because in a few years it'll be too late, if you follow me.'

'Just about,' said Lill. 'It's difficult, but I'm doing my best.'

'Specially,' concluded Guy with a leer, 'when they hurt nobody. Not, of course, that anybody'd know anyway.'

'My Fred's a terror when he's roused,' said Lill. 'You wouldn't think it to look at him, but by golly he is!'

Guy repressed a chortle of disbelief, and tensed his shoulders and arms to show off his biceps. I'd fight for you, Lill, he was saying as clearly as if he'd spoken. Lill was thrilled. She said: 'Naturally whatever I did I'd always be careful, because of Fred . . .'

The half-concession was obvious, but Guy played
his game for one more move. He put on an expression of great tenderness. 'You're lucky to have someone who really cares. I don't think my wife would
care at all, whatever I did. Ours is a funny marriage.
My wife doesn't understand me at all.'

'Blimey, she ought to,' cackled Lill, breaking the
mood. 'I understand you all right.'

'Why are we wasting time, then, eh Lill?' And Guy
Fawcett bent his heavy body urgently forward to hers
over the fence. 'Let's get on with it. Have a bit of fun
before your lot comes back for their lunch.'

Lill retreated flirtatiously to the depressing rose-
bush. 'Well, I don't say that if you come round the
back door in ten minutes with a book you'd promised
to lend me I wouldn't let you in.'

'Oh, come off it, Lill. Since when have you taken
up with literature? Nobody'd buy that even if they
heard me. I'll just hop over the fence—'

'Hey, give over you saucy bastard—' But by then
Guy Fawcett had done a one-hand spring over the
rickety fence and was approaching her with looks of
cinematic lust in his eyes. 'Hey, give over, Guy, someone might see us. Me mother—'

And at that moment Lill, in giggling mock-flight,
did turn her head round in the direction of her
mother's garden, and saw through the gap in the
straggling hedge her mother, square and aproned on
a kitchen chair, peeling potatoes in the watery sun
and regarding them with an air of malevolent dis-
approval, lips pursed, old black eyes flashing.

Lill's reaction was instantaneous and sincere: she

turned back towards the gap in the hedge and whipped her fingers into a vicious V-sign. Then she put her arm around Guy Fawcett's substantial waist, let him paw over her shoulders and round to her triumphal breasts, and so the pair went off towards the kitchen door in an ecstasy of simulated amusement. The back door was shut with tremendous emphasis, and strain as her old ears might, Mrs Casey heard no more. Lill and Fred's bedroom was at the front of the house. Shaking her head, and with a tear of shame or rage at the corners of her eyes, she put a cloth over her bowl of potatoes and slowly, arthritically, made her way back to her own kitchen.

'Penny for 'em, Fred. What are you thinking about?'

It was one of Fred's mates in the parks department who asked, coming up behind him as he filled in time before the dinner-hour in the garden around the war memorial. It was a question they often felt impelled to ask him, as he poked aimlessly around with hoe or rake, doing no good to anyone and positive harm to the newly bedded plants that before many weeks were out would spell 'Welcome to Todmarsh' in pink, yellow and blue under the names of the fallen. And when he was challenged, Fred usually replied: 'Wondering what'll win the two-thirty at Newmarket,' or 'Remembering that goal in the second half of the cup-tie last Saturday,' and then went back a little more purposefully to his work. A more honest reply would have been 'Nothing.' For in fact Fred had a tremendous capacity for letting his mind go completely blank and stay that way for hours at a time. But even Fred realized that reply would lay him open to ridicule, so he always concocted something. Today he said: 'Just thinking that if I'd got that double seven in the darts Saturday night we'd've won.'

'Oh aye,' said his mate. 'Thought you were down the Rose and Crown Saturday night with your family.'

'Only early on,' said Fred, perking up a little, and excavating energetically around a petunia which would very much rather have been left alone. 'Only early on. Couldn't let the team down.'

'Celebration, wasn't it? Birthday or summat?'

'My Gordon's twenty-sixth,' said Fred, his skinny frame swelling with pride.

'Glad he's out the army and doing well for himself. Looks a fine lad. Twenty-six, eh? Wouldn't have thought it possible, looking at your Lill.'

'No, you're right. She's a fine woman. O' course I married her young.'

'You must have, at that. Bit of a handful for you, eh Fred? Beautiful woman like that?' His mate nudged him in the ribs. 'Better keep her on a short leash, eh, or there'll be others wanting to poke your grate.' And he snickered.

Fred remained for a minute in contemplation, and then he said with the shadow of a spark: 'Hold on, Bill. I don't like you making suggestions like that.'

But by this time his mate had gone back to his work, and after looking blearily at his back for a minute or two, Fred went on with his picking and poking around the flower-beds that never came to anything very much. It would be difficult to tell whether he was deep in thought.

'Oh lumme, what are you doing?' shouted Lill, dying with laughter. 'Blimey, I never thought of that one!'

'Learn a lot when you're with me, Lill,' said Guy Fawcett, continuing what he was doing.

Mrs Casey went around her house, meticulously dusting and wiping over her relics of Leicester in the 'thirties. Then she finished the preparation for her lunch. She had been so long alone that cooking for one presented no problems for her. Today she had a little bit of cod, which she was fond of and which had become quite a treat in recent years. But now her heart wasn't in her preparations. She read her paper, but it was one that had recently been shaved down into a tabloid, and it gave her no pleasure. There are no newspapers now for the Mrs Caseys of this world. She took up her library book, but she had lost the thread of the story and failed to pick it up again. In the end she gave in, and sat before the electric fire in her front room, just staring ahead of her.

Finally, she said to herself aloud—that aloudness giving it the seal of a conclusion or a decision: 'It's a right shame. In his house too. Someone ought to tell Fred about it.'

She drew her thin lips even tighter around her old teeth, nodded her head and went out in better heart to fry her cod.

'Oh, you are a devil,' said Lill at last. 'I'd never have thought you had it in you. Quite an education, really. Just like one of those manuals you read about.'

'Quite good, eh?' agreed Guy Fawcett, relaxing on his back with an expression of sublime conceit on his face. 'Expect I could teach old Fred a thing or two.'

Lill sniggered disloyally. 'Gawd, don't mention him. I'd better go down and boil his potatoes.' For

some reason Guy sniggered in his turn. 'Here,' said
Lill, as she struggled out of bed. 'We ought to do this
more often.'

'Come back when you've put the spuds on, and we'll
see,' said Guy in a seigneurial way.

'Didn't mean that, you clot,' said Lill. And when
she returned and snuggled back against his fleshy
frame in bed she said: 'We could make this a regular
thing.'

'Tuesdays and Fridays?' said Guy. 'Regular servicing
with a stamped receipt? That's not my line, Lill, not
my line at all. I'm not the sort to get fenced in.'

'Why not?' protested Lill. 'If you enjoyed yourself . . . ?'

'Oh, I enjoyed it. But I like to play it by ear. Take
it as it comes. I'm not a boy that can work regular
hours.'

'Well, you're damned lucky your wife does,' said
Lill with spirit. 'Wonder what she'd say if I told
her.'

'Don't push your luck, Lill,' said Guy Fawcett,
pressing her shoulders brutally down against the
pillows. 'Or you'll be riding for a fall.'

'Hey, Brian,' said one of his classmates as they came
out of a period on Palmerston's foreign policy and
headed towards the long huts where dinner was served.
'Some of us are going over to Puddlesham to a disco
on Saturday night. Are you coming?'

'Saturday night?' said Brian, pushing back that
troublesome lock of hair from over his eyes. 'No,
Saturday night I've got something on.'

CHAPTER 6

COLOUR SENSE

The Coponawi Islands, which Mr Achituko had left for the drizzle and wheeze of an English winter, were dots on the map—courtesy dots at that—in the middle of the Pacific Ocean, thousands of miles from civilization, and not much nearer to Queensland. The islanders had undoubtedly been cannibal until the early eighteen-seventies, when they were Christianized by a gaunt, determined missionary, inevitably a Scot, a graduate of Edinburgh and Exeter Hall, a man so feared and respected that at his death—four years after his arrival, and before his flock could readily distinguish between Elijah and Elisha—his body was subjected to no more than the odd reverent nibble.

His flock's understanding of their new faith was at that point still wavering and nebulous, but some few could read, and when they discovered among his books (most of them too long and heavy for intellectual comfort) a little volume entitled *The Wise and Witty Sayings of George Eliot* they modelled their religion around her precepts and (in direct defiance of the good man's commands, which they easily in their minds reversed) set up wooden idols of the Sage which visiting anthropologists from Scandinavia later mistook for some form of horse worship imported by boat people from prehistoric North Africa.

Things had progressed rapidly in the Coponawi Islands since the Second World War. Nuclear tests had taken place in the vicinity and had put them on the map. Hippy colonies from California and Sydney had waxed there in the 'sixties and waned there in the 'seventies. Tourism had burgeoned, concrete blocks had risen among the coconut palms, and only the occasional disappearance of a well-fed mid-Westerner, and the subsequent discovery of sneakers or orange-feathered alpine hat had led people to wonder whether old habits didn't die hard. Mr Achituko's mind had been formed by Peace Corps volunteers, very nearly deformed at the University of Hawaii, and now he was studying cultic offshoots of the major religions at the Univerity of South Wessex, where a group of atheists and defrocked priests ran a very high-powered Comparative Religion Department. His was now a well-honed, highly sophisticated mind, though when he had recently visited the George Eliot Museum at Nuneaton the curator had been astonished to see him at various points during the guided tour performing the fourteen Stations of the Cross.

Thinking it over in bed on Saturday night, after the encounter with Lill in the Rose and Crown, Mr Achituko had been highly amused that Lill should suspect him of having designs on little Mrs Watson up the road. For in fact he was sleeping, on and off, with little Debbie Hodsden down the road, and he wouldn't have minded betting that, had she known, Lill would have been livid, not with moral outrage, but with jealousy.

Of course, it was hardly a settled thing with Debbie and could not be yet, even if Achituko decided to stay in Britain beyond the end of the academic year. His landlady was a woman of comparatively liberal mind (he had been accepted by her as a lodger after a long succession of Todmarshians had suddenly and unaccountably decided not to let rooms to students that academic year), but she had made it clear that she drew the line at miscegenational sex. 'It's not so much me,' she had explained, in fear of attracting to herself that most hated of modern labels, being called narrow-minded, 'it's what the neighbours might say. You know what people are.'

Still, Wednesday night was bingo night for her, and now and again as Spring had approached things had been possible under the inky grey skies. In the Coponawi Islands Debbie would already be a mother, and about to take on those extra rolls of flesh that were the signs of status and prosperity in those latitudes. Mr Achituko certainly did not think of himself as debauching a minor, but neither did he think of taking her with him when he returned home: he had no very high opinion of the chastity or house-keeping of English women, and it might have caused trouble with his wife and three children on the islands.

This Wednesday he was staying home to rough out a chapter of his thesis, dealing with various exciting Coptic heresies, but he had managed to exchange a couple of words with Debbie as she flew for her school bus, and he felt the day was likely to be a satisfying mixture of the sacred and the profane. However his sally to the gate had been observed, and when his landlady came to clear away his breakfast things she

lingered meaningfully, and finally said: 'Quite friendly with the Hodsdens, aren't you?'

'So-so,' said Mr Achituko, flashing his irresistible
black and white smile. 'I see them sometimes in the
Rose and Crown.'

'So I heard,' said Mrs Evangeline Carstairs (Eve to
her friends), a considerable, opinionated and not un-
attractive woman whose husband worked in Bristol
and was generally only to be seen at weekends, exhausted by work, Mrs Carstairs and British Rail. 'Of
course, it's just a matter of taste, isn't it?'

'You dislike them, do you?' asked Achituko, who
preferred to come out into the open with her, since
her opinions were pithier when there were no polite
manœuvrings.

'Oh, the children are all right,' said Eve Carstairs,
crashing plates and saucers around on the tray.
'Though if you ask me, the boys are a poor-spirited lot
to put up with it the way they do . . .' She ostentatiously said no more.

'But the parents—?'

'Well, you couldn't say anything against Fred, I
suppose, because there's really nothing there, is there?
More like a tadpole than what I'd call a man. But
her—if you ask me she lets the road down and has
since the day she came here. She's common as dirt,
and if you believe half of what you hear around
town, she's got the morals of an alley cat with it!'

'Really?' said Mr Achituko, who in fact knew infinitely more about Lill's activities than Mrs Carstairs.
'I must admit that at times I find her a little—embarrassing.'

'Don't we all? 'Course, you've got the colour thing
with it, which makes it worse. Still, it's that daughter

of hers I feel really sorry for: you feel it at that age.
I expect Debbie does, doesn't she?'

She looked at him with a knowing air.

'Very likely,' said Achituko noncommittally. He
wondered for a moment if—were things to come out
into the open—Mrs Carstairs would be persuaded to
give her blessing to his activities with Debbie. But,
wisely, he remembered her age and refrained. And in
fact Mrs Carstairs had quite other things on her
mind, for as she took the tray out she said:

'If I was the girl I'd leave town as soon as I could.
Get a job somewhere—she's not stupid. But nobody
around here who knew the mother would want anything to do with the daughter. Whatever they say,
there's such a thing as bad blood!'

For Eve Carstairs did not look with favour on Mr
Achituko's choice. After all, she was herself a woman
in the prime of life, magnificently fleshed, and in all
the time he had been there Achituko had come no
closer to the personal than to praise her Yorkshire
puddings.

'What were you and Achituko talking about?' asked
Brian as he and Debbie climbed breathless on to the
school bus.

'Just passing the time of day,' said Debbie. 'Get off
my back, will you?' And she went up front and sat
with her friends, where they talked about various
spotty and loud-mouthed youths whom her friends
fancied and Debbie felt she was now infinitely too
experienced to contemplate seriously. But she hugged
her secret to herself, and gave bored attention to the
discussion of the finer points of these adolescents.

Brian sat in the back seat of the upper deck, sur-

rounded by his fellow sixth-formers touching up
their last night's prep. But after a minute or two
Brian, remembering that encounter between Debbie
and Achituko at the Carstairs' gate, went off into a
dream. Was there something between those two? No—
couldn't possibly be. Debbie was much too young.
Still, there *were* girls who . . . he knew there were
girls that age at the High School who . . . But Debbie
wasn't the type. She was just an ordinary schoolgirl.
He'd seen her grow up. Now Lill at that age! . . .
She'd once told a story about herself at sixteen, an
encounter with the shop-floor manager of the cuddly-
toy factory in Leicester where she had worked . . . 'Oh,
he *was* a saucy one!' Lill had ended, having got herself and him into the works canteen after the rest
had knocked off. Brian had laughed with the rest, and
later he had gone up and been sick in the bathroom.

He remembered Lill in Tunisia . . . Why was it
always Tunisia? . . . He remembered Lill and the
middle-aged German with the bulbous body like a
potter's discard . . . the way he lingered heavily round
them by the swimming-pool in the first days, the way
he started buying Lill expensive drinks, pawing her
when Fred was not around, uttering guttural endear-
ments and giggling obscenities when the younger ones
went off into the pool . . .

He remembered Lill on the beach, surrounded by
the sellers of bangles and pots and rugs and sunhats—
swarthy men and boys, haphazardly clad, men the
other English declared were terrible pests and waved
away, fearful of being swindled. But Lill had welcomed them, and chattered away to them in pidgin
Midlands, admiring their wares, trying them on, ex-

acting their homage, now and then fetching out her purse and buying one of the pots that now sat unsteadily on the mantelpieces and coffee-tables around the house (the pot-seller had been young, younger than her sons, and doe-eyed, and wicked). Lill had lapped it up. 'They think I'm marvelous,' she would announce at dinner. 'Nobody else will talk to them, stuck-up lot. I could fancy one or two of them too, even if they are wogs! I wish they'd come selling things round my back door at home!'

And he remembered the boys that day he and Gordon had walked alone into Hammamet, the boys who ran after them as they lounged around the medina, laughing, prancing, joking and shouting—shouting *'Voulez-vous coucher avec ma sœur?'* and then . . .

'Here wake up, dreamy,' said the boy next to him. 'I want to read your answer to the question on *Lord of the Flies.*'

As luck would have it, Lill and Mrs Carstairs found themselves alone behind the butcher's counter that morning, Lill waiting to buy a pound and a half of snags, while Eve Carstairs bought some nice kidney chops.

'That's right,' yelled Lill, with that unconsciousness of her effect on others that was her hallmark and her death-warrant, 'you feed up my Archie. Don't want my lover-boy wasting away.'

Mrs Carstairs compressed her lips, looked straight across the counter at the butcher with an expression of conspiratorial long-suffering, and said: 'Nobody can say I don't give my lodgers good value.'

'Hope you get good value in exchange, then,' said

Lill with a squawk of laughter. 'Lucky old you, that's what I say. I got a taste for darkies in Tunisia.'

Perhaps she touched a raw emotional nerve in Eve Carstairs, perhaps it was the butcher's presence, so obviously enjoying himself, that made Eve take her up on something she ordinarily would have contemptuously passed over. At any rate, she wheeled round with whiplash suddenness and said: 'And what is that supposed to imply?'

Lill laughed on cheerily, regardless of anger or opposition: 'Oh, no offence. I'd give a quid for your luck. If my hubby was away all week like yours I'd have a couple of darkies—one for my bed and a reserve in the spare room!'

Eve Carstairs exploded. 'If you want to know who is sleeping with Achituko, you'd best go and ask your own daughter,' she spat, and flounced from the shop.

Gordon Hodsden, cycling home from the shipyard that Wednesday at five, saw Ann Watson walking with her little girl towards the recreation ground. He rode up beside the kerb in front of her and stood waiting till she came up, straddled across his bike.

'I say, I'm sorry if my mum's been round your place saying things, and that. She gets ideas in her head, you know, but she doesn't mean any harm.'

Ann Watson, looking at him—his appealing smile, his obvious good-will, his chunky presentability—nevertheless felt her anger at Lill spurting up anew. 'Well, she ought to be careful,' she said. 'People like her do a lot of harm, even if they don't intend to.'

'But you can't tell my mum that,' said Gordon, widening that disingenuous smile. 'If she thinks a thing she goes ahead and says it. It's not her fault, really, it's what she's like. All she wants is to help people.'

'Sometimes it's best not to interfere,' said Ann Watson, almost rudely indicating she wanted to be off. 'People are better off left to themselves.'

'Oh, Mum has to do her little bit—wouldn't be happy otherwise,' said Gordon gaily. 'Well, just thought I'd say something. Hope there's no hard feelings.'

And he rode off, apparently unconscious of the fact that there was no reply. But as he rode, his face darkened into an expression as unlike that open, smiling boyishness as it could possibly be, and, lowering and heavily thoughtful, he pedalled furiously the last stretch of the way home. Well, that's cooked my goose with *her*, he thought. She wouldn't give a second thought to someone as stupid as I made myself out to be. All in a good cause, though. There'll be time to bring her round—afterwards.

'What do you think about when my mother goes on like she did on Saturday night?' asked Debbie of Mr Achituko as they lay, close and cosy, in his single bed at No. 38 at nine o'clock that evening.

'Think about? As little as possible. I just let it wash over me,' said Achituko, shrugging his fleshy shoulders.

'Yes, but when she goes on about your colour and whether it washes off and all that sort of stuff, like she does all the time. It had me cringing. I mean you must react to that, surely. It's about your skin—about *you*.'

Achituko leaned over her lean, adolescent body and drew his brown finger down her cheek. 'Does yours come off? Do I get white chalk marks all over my finger? No, it doesn't. And you don't get annoyed, do you?'

Debbie giggled. 'That's different. You're not Lill. Anyway, I'm white. Nobody . . . nobody despises whites.'

I do, I do, thought Achituko. But he merely smiled his wide, open smile at her naivety.

'I'd love to have seen you give her a tremendous slosh round the chops,' said Debbie, with relish. 'I was sitting there hoping for it. That's what I'm going to do before very long, one day when she really gets my goat.'

'You'd better wait, little fire-cracker,' said Achituko. 'She's a tough customer, your mother. Better wait till you're a little older. Or leave it to me to do, when she finds out about us.'

'Just so long as I'm there,' said Debbie, with a childish, anticipatory smile. 'But I wish you'd done it on Saturday. That'd have stopped her going on about how she loves wogs.'

'You've got a violent nature, you know that, girl?' And Achituko lay there chuckling happily, cuddling her to him, his eyes dark and thoughtful in the shadowy bedroom.

Outside in the darkness, as far as possible from the streetlamps and sheltered by an overhanging apple tree, Lill waited silently, puffing on a rolled cigarette which she hid in the palm of her cupped hand. There were no lights in Eve Carstairs's house, and not a sound emerging. She had loitered past earlier, twice, but had not heard a whisper. And yet, surely, if they made love there at any time, it must be Wednesday nights. When Eve Carstairs invariably went to bingo. Lill's lip curled. Normally she herself would be at bingo tonight. Very convenient for the little slut, she thought: both mother and landlady out. She only kicked herself that she had let Debbie disappear after tea without following her. No doubt she had gone off to a friend's, then come back here later. It hadn't been practicable to keep a constant watch until night had fallen. In half an hour Mrs Carstairs would be on her way home. Debbie would be well out of the house by then, if she had any sense. Twenty minutes more and she'd give up.

She stiffened. A light went on momentarily in the hall of 38, then off again, but in those two seconds she had seen two shapes through the lead-lighted window in the front door. Now the door was opening silently, now there were muttered intimacies—Lill ground her cigarette under her heel savagely—now a dark shape was through the tiny front garden, out through the gate, and off down the road in the other direction. Lill left the shadow of the Cox's Orange and hared off after it. Sure enough, the shadow turned into No. 10, and she heard her own back door open and shut.

Now she threw off all disguise or stealth. Charging forward, she flung open the gate and crashed through the front door, nearly bowling over Debbie, taking off her coat by the clothes-peg in the hall.

'Oh, hello, Mum—' her daughter began.

Lill seized her by the arm, her purpled fingernails biting into the flesh, and pushed her bodily through to the kitchen. Once there she threw her across the room with such passionate force that she landed crying over the sink. Lill banged the kitchen door and stood against it, arms on her hips, her face blotched with jealousy and hate.

'Now, my girl,' she said, 'I'm going to make you regret what you've just been doing.'

CHAPTER 7

THURSDAY

Thursday breakfast was a meal on tenterhooks. Lill stood tight-lipped over the stove and boiled eggs on principles of guesswork. The family scurried down one after the other, gobbled their under- or over-done free-ranges, and then dived out of the kitchen and went about their business. Debbie came down defiantly, the whiteness of her face emphasizing the blue bruise around her left eye and the cut on the side of her mouth. When she said disgustedly, 'This egg's hardly done at all,' the rest of the family shushed her agitatedly, as if she were tempting the wrath of the Almighty. Unconcerned, she pushed the egg aside and helped herself to toast and marmalade. She did not try to conceal the fact that she was eating with difficulty. Lill could hardly bear to look at her. But when she got up from the table Lill rounded on her and snapped:

'You're not going to school. Not like that.'

Debbie gave her a long, cool, impertinent look, but then said: 'All right.'

Ten minutes later, though, she hared down from her bedroom, whipped her coat off the peg in the hall, and was out the front door in a flash meticulously timing it so as to catch the bus by a hairsbreadth and avoid pursuit and capture. All Lill could do was stand by the front gate and glower at her retreating figure.

'Forget something, did she?' said Mrs Forsdyke from No. 18, passing in the other direction. 'These teenagers are all alike, aren't they?'

'You can say that again,' snarled Lill. 'Bloody little slut, I'll teach her.'

Not quite sure she had heard, Mrs Forsdyke smiled vaguely and went on her way, but the conviction gradually came over her that Mrs Hodsden had called her daughter a bloody little slut, and the expression on Lill's face convinced her that All Was Not Well with the Hodsdens. Since she served in the best greengrocer's in Todmarsh she had plenty of chances to communicate this conviction to half the town, including many of her neighbours in Windsor Avenue and the surrounding streets, before the morning was out. Her news, conveyed in a hushed whisper, like a royal scandal, met with a series of raised eyebrows. 'Really's,' 'I don't wonder's,' and 'How that family puts up with her I don't know's'. Uniquely, nobody sympathized with the parent. Because Lill was not loved in her neighbourhood.

Nor did she do anything to make herself loved that morning. Lill spoiling for a row was one thing: that was a variety of good mood. Lill in a black, destructive temper was quite another thing, and infinitely more frightening. Her plans were in ruin, her self-love had received a blow, the arrangement of her world, that elegant construction of castles in the air peopled by admiring dummies, had been flattened by a brutal kick. Lill was livid. She felt within her a dull, throbbing, continuous rage—or, as she put it, she felt all churned up. And it was clear that someone, several people, had to get hurt. That was only right.

She began the day as she meant to go on. In the garden that backed on to her own children were playing hide-and-seek with squeals of excitement. Seeing the mother at the door, Lill marched down to her back fence and bellowed: 'Can't you keep those bloody kids quiet? I can't hear myself think in there. They're a public menace.' Ten minutes later she swaggered round next door to 'have it out' with her mother. Only in her most brutal moods could Lill hope to win such a contest, but by the end of half an hour the redoubtable Mrs Casey was close to tears. Finally Lill banged out of the back door with an expression of grim triumph on her face, and turning back, she shouted:

'And if you're thinking of sneaking to Fred, you can give up the idea. I've told him about it myself, so put that in your pipe. There's going to be some changes around here before long, I'm telling you, and you're not going to like them.'

It wasn't the last brush of the day with one or other of her natural enemies. Meeting Guy Fawcett's wife slipping home from work at mid-morning, she roared: 'Christ, some people have it lucky. Get paid for doing nothing. But I suppose you've got to check up on that randy husband of yours.'

Mrs Fawcett looked at her with open contempt before slipping in through her front gate. Once safely inside she said: 'I've given up worrying what Guy was up to long ago.'

'Haven't got much choice, I shouldn't think,' said Lill, with ferocious directness. 'Need a red-hot poker to put him out of action.'

'I expect you'd know,' said Jane Fawcett, going into the house and banging the front door.

News of Lill's mood spread along Windsor Avenue like a thick, stinking cloud from a burning chemical plant. As she went by people watched from well within the shadows of their front rooms, and decided not to go down the street until she was safely back home. Poor old Miss Gaitskell, retired post-mistress, bulky and all too aware of it, had not sensed the cloud and was unwittingly weeding her front garden as Lill strode past. She did not entirely register the relevance of the remark 'Blimey, if I had an arse like that, I wouldn't bend over' until Lill was well past her, but when she did she straightened, flushed, and looked indignantly at the retreating leopard-skin coat. In the course of Lill's daily round the butcher was flayed, the newsagent was flattened. It wasn't that Lill's remarks were acute, but if the aim is to annihilate, the meat-axe is more effective than the scalpel.

Dinner with Fred and Gordon was not a happy meal. Even Gordon, the beloved son, felt the rough side of her tongue. They shovelled the food in, swilled down a mug of tea each, and then mumbled excuses to get out of the house.

Tea was worse. Debbie came home from school exhilarated by the support of her friends, self-congratulatory about the air of sad mystery she had assumed when commiserated with by her teachers. Her defiance was by now almost perky. It rubbed up Lill the wrong way like a pen-nib on the bottom of an ink bottle. Instinct told her that—as with her mother —brutality was the only sure weapon now. 'I'll teach you to defy me, you little cow,' she shrieked, and

grabbing her by the arms she dragged her upstairs—
'Gordon!' screamed Debbie, but Gordon didn't come
—and threw her into her room. Grabbing at the key,
she banged the door and locked it noisily. 'And there
you stay,' she yelled. 'And not a bite of food do you
get till I give the say-so.' She marched downstairs.

'It's about time that girl had a bit of discipline,'
she said with something approaching self-satisfaction.
'She'll feel the weight of my hand tomorrow if I have
a squeak out of her. She's been let run wild.' She
looked daggers at Fred, as if it were all his fault, and
threw him the key. 'It's your job to see she stays
there all evening. Keep your wits about you. Don't go
dozing in front of the telly like you usually do.'

'If the girl's locked in—' began Fred.

'She's sharper than a wagon-load of monkeys,'
snapped Lill. 'She'll be out of that window or I don't
know what if you don't keep a sharp watch-out. So
STAY AWAKE—I'm warning you!'

And she went off to get the tea. Something during
that scene had clicked in the back of Brian's head,
and it refused to come forward. It worried him. Or
was he just worried by his failure to stand up for his
sister? Fred also looked unhappy, and slipped out of
the front door to prod futilely at the rambling rose
climbing feebly up a trellis, perhaps with the vague
idea of seeing if Debbie could climb down that way.
When he had wandered wraithlike from the front
room Gordon, on his way upstairs to wash and change,
hissed to Brian: 'Garry Prior's having a bachelor
party at the Rose and Crown tonight. Registry Office
do in the morning, hurried. I said we'd go. It'll be the
last dry run before the killing.'

Something still tugged obstinately at the back of Brian's mind. He said: 'I hardly know Garry Prior. You go, he's your age. He won't want me there.'

'Without you it won't be a rehearsal, you idiot. I said you'd be there.' He winked. 'He's a bit down. Caught, like. The more the merrier.' And he bounded up the stairs to get out of his overalls and to soap away the rasp of work from his hands.

Downstairs, languidly flicking through the pages of a dated history book, Brian was suddenly struck by the revelation which had been struggling to come out all day. Was it revelation, or self-deception? Debbie's black eye, seen and discussed in Todmarsh and at school, had surely ditched their whole scheme. They'd been relying on the happy-family Hodsden image, and now—for the moment, anyway—that had been shattered. Kill Lill now and you only landed Debbie in it. Kill Lill now, and the whole family was in it. The first people the police would be looking at. The more he examined the idea, the more the impossibility of their plan struck him. They could not kill Lill! Not on Saturday. Not ever. A great wave of nauseous relief washed over him. They were stuck with her, but they were not going to be her killers. He'd have to hammer it into Gordon's thick skull somehow. He'd discuss it with him in bed tonight. He felt elated with a sense of—of what? Freedom? No, not that. Then could it be relief at the continuance of his bondage?

Lill was full of grim triumph at tea-time, and read the riot act to her men.

'That little slut's not to have a bite of food until she's come round, right? I'll give you what for, Fred, if you slip up with anything while I'm out tonight.

Same goes for you two—and I don't want you talking to her at the door either. Silence and starvation—that'll bring her round. I'll have her crawling for forgiveness by Saturday.'

'Better not keep her away from school too long, Mum,' said Brian. 'You'll have the authorities on to you. They must have noticed the bruise.'

Lill looked at him in outrage. 'Cheeky bugger. I'd like to see the school inspector that would interfere between me and my daughter. I'd soon settle his hash if he tried.'

Brian kept quiet, because Lill spoke no less than the truth. And Gordon snarled inwardly at the whole episode, but told himself he'd soon be doing Debbie more good than ever he could by standing up for her now. And, after all, she had asked for it.

At the usual time Lill gathered herself together, slapped on make-up more crudely even than usual, and announced her departure.

'I'm just off to see Mrs Corby. Now mind what I said, Fred. You're to have nothing to do with that girl whatsoever. And you drop off in front of that set and I'll skin you alive.'

'No, Lill, I'll remember.'

Lill banged out of the front door and out through the front gate. But she did not get far along Windsor Avenue, since as ill-luck would have it she nearly ran into Mr Achituko, strolling amiably past. Alone of Windsor Avenue he knew nothing about 'something being up' at the Hodsdens'. Only Eve Carstairs would be likely to tell him, and she as it happened had felt a twinge of guilt when she heard of the nebulous 'trouble', and wondered whether she might not be herself responsible. So Mr Achituko was surprised (though not entirely bewildered about the cause) when he found himself grabbed by the lapels of his immaculately cut suit and found Lill's eyes—bulbous, black, outraged—two inches from his own, part of a general expression of murderous malevolence.

'Listen to me, you bloody black stud. No, don't pretend you don't know what I mean. I know what you and Debbie have been up to. And I tell you this: I'll have the law on you if you so much as touch her again—do you hear? I'm not having a nigger son-in-law and coffee-coloured grandchildren. You say one word to my daughter, ever in the future, and I'll get your licence revoked!'

And she let go his lapels and marched off down the road in triumph. Mr Achituko, patting his suit back into its pristine smartness, restrained his desire to run after her and do her some modest violence. Mentally he translated Lill's last phrase into a threat to have his temporary residence permit withdrawn. Ludicrous as the threat was, he knew enough about the police and immigration officials to know that people—blacks—had been expelled for infinitely more trivial or idiotic reasons. He stood in the street, dignity outraged and unrevenged, and felt very far from happy. Then, setting his face back into its usual amiable grin in case he was watched, he wheeled round and marched dignifiedly in the opposite direction.

On the way down to the Rose and Crown, Gordon was obsessed, as he had been since Saturday, with his plan of campaign. So bright, intent, absorbed was he that Brian hadn't the heart to argue the toss with him, to throw in doubt the whole plan. Gordon was a boy again, fighting global battles with toy soldiers.

It was all a matter of tactics, strategy, logistics, reduced to a tiny scale.

'Then sometime in the evening,' he finished up, 'I'll disappear. I'll be doing it tonight—so notice. Strictly twelve minutes, or perhaps a minute or two over, to be on the safe side. I'll just stay in the bog this time. Just go on as usual, talk, notice whether I'm missed. But I won't be—no chance. There's a whole crowd coming tonight, and it'll be just like a Saturday.'

'When it comes down to it, it's not much of an alibi,' remarked Brian.

'It's good enough. There's nobody can prove I wasn't there at the crucial time. Nobody remembers a blind thing on a Saturday evening, when things have got going. It'll be the same tonight.'

And certainly Garry Prior and his mates seemed determined to make quite a do of it. The cynicism behind the gaiety added an extra note of frenzy to the occasion. Half the shipyard seemed to be there, and a whole group that ten years ago had been a loud-mouthed motor-cycle gang, terrorizing roadside pubs and rendering respectable neighbourhoods hideous with their din, now sunk into a world of nappies, baked bean suppers and querulous wives.

Gordon fitted naturally into this mob, knew the indecent songs that ought to be sung on such occasions, had the inevitable follow-up remarks to the inevitable jokes at his tongue's end. Brian was at first diffident, with that feeling of apartness which is the great achievement of the English grammar school. He watched the clumsy, jolly men pretending to be boys and wondered what he could find to say to them. But little by little the barriers of ice were melted by

the warm beer, and Brian found he could join in
the choruses of the songs, swing his mug joyously at
the crucial obscenities, and throw back his head and
roar at jokes that he had trained himself to find crude
or sexist. He was feeling, through his whole body, not
fellow-feeling, but the lifting of a weight the lighten-
ing of his future, a great sense of freedom-in-captivity.

We can't do it now, he periodically told himself.
Now it would come straight back on the family.
Gordon's got to see that.

So happy was he that he failed to notice when or
whether Gordon left the bar, how long he was away,
or whether anyone noticed. But he was light-headed
with relief: it didn't matter now. They would never
do it. Lill had won through again, he thought, and
wondered how long he would be happy that she had.

Fred sat bolt upright in his chair at No. 10, Windsor
Avenue, consciously on guard like a meticulous sheep-
dog. One thing he was not going to do tonight was
go to sleep. He wondered whether he might take a bite
to eat up to Debbie in her room. His consideration
of this topic was a mere matter of form, something
to think about: he knew he would not dare. Lill had
said he wasn't to, and he wouldn't. He watched the
beginning of an episode of a Francis Durbridge serial,
and tried to make head or tail of the mysterious
phone calls, the multiple identities, the inexplicable
goings-on in the stockbroker belt. It took his mind off
Debbie for the moment, but he came back to her. No
doubt Lill was right. She always was. And what the
girl had done was shocking—real disgusting. He
played with the idea of sexual licence, and felt a
vague pang of unease somewhere at the back of his

head. No—he wouldn't take a bite up to Debbie. He'd do as Lill had told him. Naturally he would. He settled down into his usual rut of non-thought . . .

Suddenly he shook himself. The Francis Durbridge was over, and he hardly remembered a thing that had happened in it. Must watch out. He'd nearly dropped off then.

The evening at the Rose and Crown developed as such evenings do. By ten o'clock the bridegroom-to-be was in a state that could only be described as off-putting, but of course the bride was not there to be put off. Red, sweaty, distended and bulbous of eye, he was alternately raucous and maudlin, and resisted all attempts by his more responsible mates to get him home to bed. 'It's my last night,' he kept saying, as though the hangman were coming for him in the cold quiet early hours.

As far as Brian could tell—and he was pretty high now, with drink and relief—Gordon was mixing with dazzling virtuosity among the various groups: a word here, a joke there, hands on shoulders for a rugby song elsewhere. It was a marvel: he was everywhere, and yet nowhere in particular. He's keyed up, thought Brian, exhilarated by the thought of Saturday, just as I'm relieved we won't be doing anything. The thought suddenly depressed him again. How long before the project came up for discussion once more, even if they did shelve it for the present? And Brian had a sudden stab of fear that Gordon never would consent to shelve it. He was emotionally committed, and for all his apparently cool tactical planning, Gordon ran on his emotions. What if the thing went ahead after all? Fear now was back with him, back with that iron grip on his stomach it had had all week, making ominous rollings among the beer. But even if Gordon got caught and jailed, he told himself through a haze of drink and uncertainty, they could never pin anything on him, Brian. That was what was so humiliating in a way: his part in the whole thing amounted to nothing plus, and that was why nothing could be pinned on him. And then, if Gordon went to jail, for a long, long sentence . . . The thought of life without Lill or Gordon sent that strange pang of longing and fear through him again. It would be freedom. But could he cope with freedom?

On one of his bee-like hops from group to group Gordon found Brian temporarily alone, and stopped.

'How did it go? Anyone notice I was gone?'

'No. Nobody would, not in this shambles. Gord, there's something I want to say—'

'Not here, you fool. The mugs have ears.' And with a smile in which only Brian could detect signs of strain Gordon sailed into his next all-boys-together encounter.

And now it was all songs. You had to end the evening with a song, didn't you? And then another. The plasticated imitation oak rafters rang, and Methodist households streets away shut their windows and doors. The beer-loosened voices rose in ecstatically scatological songs of praise, and in the unholy din Brian did not hear the phone ring in the landlord's little den behind the bar, or see him disappear into it. But minutes later he registered with bleary surprise the figure of the landlord coming round the bar with an odd, unaccustomed expression of worry and uncertainty in his face and bearing—not like Jack Perkins, life and soul of the party except with his wife and kids. And Brian saw him enquiring something of one or two of the less drunk, saw him move towards Gordon, saw him bring him over, heard him say through the haze of beer and song and smoky bonhomie:

'Look, I'm sorry, you boys, I've just had a message—you'd better—well, you'd better cut off home—it's rather serious—it's your mum—she's—'

'Ill?'

'Well, sort of, but worse. I'm sorry, lads. They say she's dead. I couldn't hear right well, you know, not through all this. But they said she'd been killed.'

Brian felt Gordon keel over towards him, crumpling at the knees and up the strong trunk of his body. Then with a powerful effort he righted himself, clutched on to the table uttering great racking sobs. Suddenly he cried 'Killed!' and then shoved his way bodily through the crowd and out of the bar door. Brian ran in his wake and followed him in his first fast sprint up Balaclava Road. Two hundred yards from the pub Gordon stopped by the lamppost and heaved mountainously and noisily. And as Brian caught him up and stood over him, helpless, Gordon gazed at him through his heaving and retching, his face blotched hideously red, his eyes wet with grief and disappointment, and said:

'Some bastard's gone and done it instead o' me. She was mine. I had it all worked out, you know that, down to the last detail. Some bastard's got there first. Now I'll never be able to throttle the life out of her.'

'Come on,' hissed Brian, shaking himself into taking control. 'He said she'd been killed. He probably meant an accident. Don't crack up.'

And with a last mountainous heave and a shake Gordon did seem to get a grip, stood up, took out a handkerchief and wiped his eyes. Then he took off like a professional sprinter up the dark road. He faltered a little as they ploughed their way through the blackness of Snoggers Alley, and Brian caught him up so that together they could run the last stretch home.

Home. Lill's nest for her boys. But now transformed with lights, with two large police cars outside, and with a little knot of shameless neighbours and their children, watching the comings and goings. They made way for Gordon and Brian, gazed at them with ravenous, awkwardly respectful curiosity, stayed silent as they pushed their way through the front gate.

And Brian's most abiding memory of the day was the open front door, the hall blazing with light, and Fred meeting them, his skinny frame racked with sobs, his face red with rage and grief, tears running down his wrinkled cheeks, his voice cracked with shock and outrage.

'Somebody's done her in,' he shouted. 'Some bugger's been and killed our Lill.'

CHAPTER 8

THE MORNING AFTER

Morning. Waking. A dull sense of activity around the house. A sense of policemen in the house. Heavy feet and low, muffled voices. The aftermath of a murder.

Brian struggled to consciousness through a thick blanket of reluctance, hangover, and sense of impending disaster. It was seven o'clock. He had had, perhaps, five hours' sleep. He and Gordon, long, long after midnight, and after questions dimly understood and haltingly answered, after cups of thick black instant coffee, had staggered up the stairs and—silent, almost, uncertain where they stood—had thrown themselves on to their beds and sunk into welcome, immediate oblivion.

Or not quite oblivion. Brian had had terrifying dreams of Lill, blue, strangulated, hideous, dead but still active, stalking the house where once she had reigned intent on revenge. He knew too that Gordon had cried out in the night without knowing how he knew. A sharp cry of pain or triumph. Lill was there in his sleep too. Of course she was. What else could one expect? Demons are not to be exorcized so easily.

In the next bedroom Fred, similarly wafting towards consciousness, turned his meagre, flannel-py-

jamaed frame over in the bed and felt the space where
Lill always slept. It was empty. Good old Lill, he
thought: she's making the tea. Then he struggled upright, his thin body racked by coughs till tears came
to his eyes.

Next door Mrs Casey lay wakeful in bed. Now that
she was old she found she needed very little sleep.
She lay in bed most nights thinking about her life,
about what the Lord had given her and what He
had withheld, about the lives and doings of her family and neighbours, about sin and retribution and
kindred subjects. She was never bored. Last night
after she had heard, she had thought about her
daughter, about her life and death, so perfectly in ac-
cord with each other, and no doubt ordained that way
by a Higher Power. She imagined Lill's face blue
with strangulation, then remembered it thick with
pancake make-up, mascara and lipstick. There was a
rightness about the comparison that pleased her and
brought a thin smile to her face. Lill had lived vilely
and died violently. Mrs Casey stolidly turned back
the bedclothes and began the process of getting up.
Now no doubt there would be interviews and questions. The police would be round. That was only
right. They had their jobs to do. But she did not expect them to discover the murderer of Lill. She had
an odd idea that the murderer of Lill enjoyed the
protection of the Lord.

The Hodsdens gathered downstairs, haggard, pale
grey around the eyes. Debbie's right eye had something more than mere greyness round it, and she felt
the flick of an eye as one of the policemen noticed

it. That was the new policeman, the one from Cumbledon, come to take over the investigation.

They all looked at him, the one who had not been there in the horrible, frenzied session late the previous night. He's very good-looking, Debbie thought. And he was too, in a self-conscious way. Very fair hair, damped down close around his head. Blue eyes—so much more policeman-like than brown. A rounded, regular sort of face on a sturdy neck. He looks a capable sort of chap, thought Fred. He coughed portentously and came forward to shake him by the hand.

'We're all hoping you're goin' to find the rotten bastard that killed our Lill,' he said.

The policeman nodded, rather superior. Of course he was going to find the bastard that killed their Lill, seemed to be his message. Brian suddenly thought: he looks *stupid*. He hides it well, but really he's rather dim. Brian analysed his feelings, not quite sure whether to be glad or sorry. One thing he was certain of: he did want to know who it was had killed Lill. That didn't mean he wanted them punished.

The policeman cleared his throat and looked around him, using his clear, blue, frank eyes in a way he often practised in front of the bathroom mirror. Female shoplifters often went weak at the knees and confessed in the face of that gaze. The Hodsdens looked suitably impressed, which gratified him.

'My name is McHale,' he said, in a voice resonant with officialdom. 'I've been called in to take charge of this case. Believe me, I realize what a distressing time this must be for you. But I expect you'd like to know how far we've got.'

'Aye, we would that,' said Fred, who seemed anxious to make an impression on McHale as head of the family, something he never had been.

'Well, as you know, your wife—your mother—was strangled along Balaclava Road, just up from the little cutting that takes you through to Windsor Avenue here.'

'Snoggers Alley, that's what we calls it,' said Fred.

'Really . . . ?' (The pause suggested he found the Hodsdens rather common.) 'Where she was strangled there's a garden wall jutting out on to the pavement, making a dark little corner. It's very likely the murderer hid himself there—if he aimed to surprise her, that is, which seems likely. The killing took place, we would imagine, somewhere between eight-thirty and ten past ten, when the body was found. Any questions?'

'Can't they be more exact than that, these doctors?' asked Fred. 'It's so vague, anyone could have done it.'

'No, it's only in books the doctors are willing to be so exact about the time of death. But no doubt as time goes by we'll narrow it down by other methods.' Chief Inspector McHale oozed self-confidence. 'Now, just one or two more details: Mrs Hodsden's handbag was open and her purse had been ransacked—it was empty, in fact. Was there likely to have been much in it?'

'We're not rich folks,' said Fred.

We are poor, but we are honest, thought Brian, victims of old Lily's whims . . . What's Fred up to, answering all these questions as if he was somebody? He's a changed man. Lill's death has gone to his head.

Perhaps Gordon thought the same, for he spoke for

the first time: 'Mum never had much on her, and she wouldn't have had last night, not on a Thursday. She'd have got the housekeeping on Friday . . . today.'

'Makes you think,' said Fred, gazing ahead.

An expression of irritation crossed McHale's bland, handsome face, as if he were used to a better class of murder victim. 'At any rate,' he said, 'what there was in the purse is gone. We'll also have to ask you to look at the contents of Mrs Hodsden's handbag to see if anything else is missing.'

'What sort of things?' asked Fred.

'Oh . . . valuables . . . you know . . .'

Fred shook his head, bewilderedly. 'We're ordinary folks,' he said.

Christ, thought Brian. Somebody ought to offer us starring roles in *The Diary of a Nobody*. Fred Pooter and all the junior Pooters. Aloud he said:

'Mum was very careful: she wouldn't have carried anyhing valuable around with her.' Like the latest tray of diamond trinkets sent on approval from Cartier's, the Farbergé Easter eggs she had purchased from an impoverished survivor of the Russian Imperial family. My God, I can't stand it. If Fred's going to go through this investigation waggling the banner of our ordinariness I'll have to put him down. At least before we were Lill's brood, objects of pity mingled with contempt. By the time the murder fuss has died down we'll be nothing minus, if Fred has his way.

It seemed as if Fred couldn't keep himself quiet. He said greedily: 'What did the bugger strangle her with?'

'Probably wire,' said McHale with reluctance and

some distaste. 'A length of wire. There may have been some sort of makeshift handle on the ends, so he could grip it better.'

Brian felt sick. In fact, all but Debbie looked green. Lill had been garrotted. They shifted uneasily in their chairs and gazed at the floor.

'Well,' said McHale, putting on an expression of deep sympathy and beginning to collect his things together. 'There's nothing much I can say, is there? You have my deepest sympathy, but the best service I can do for you is to get the chap who did it, as you say. I'm afraid I'll have to talk to you all later, at the Station. I don't think at the moment there's anything more I can do here.'

'Will we be able to get the funeral over soon?' said Debbie suddenly.

McHale shot a quick, surprised look at her, then smoothed over his features into their habitual officially bland expression. 'I'm afraid that won't be possible until after the inquest. I hope that won't be too long hence.'

'Awful to think of her lying there—like that—in that morgue,' said Fred mournfully, wiping away a feeble tear. 'That's what's worrying our Debbie—isn't it, Debbie?'

After a pause Debbie nodded. It was half the truth. Until Lill was buried, burned, disposed of away from mortal sight, she still had a horrible marginal existence. She was still *here*. Debbie wanted her underground. Then her liberation would be complete, and she could begin the business of life, unshackled . . .

'I'll call you in, then, when I want you,' said McHale, 'and I hope you'll all be thinking about this, trying to put your finger on something that might be of use to us.' He once more indulged in his sweeping look around the assembled Hodsdens and their ineradicably lower-middle-class front room, then took himself self-importantly out. Left on their own, they looked at each other, feeling somehow truncated, and found they had nothing to say. Finally Fred cleared his throat and said: 'Well, we'd better all lend a hand with the breakfast, and then I'll be off to work.'

'Oh, for God's sake, Fred,' exploded Gordon. 'You don't go to *work* on the day your wife dies!'

Fred looked bewildered. It was Friday. A working day. What was one to do if one didn't go to work? 'I suppose I could prick out those petunias out the back,' he said.

Where were they to talk? Over breakfast—interrupted by policemen coming in and out of the back door and marching all over the house on odd errands—the problem exerted both Brian and Gordon, and they threw significant glances in each other's direction over Debbie's scrambled eggs. A strange fear gripped the two of them: they felt watched, spied on, overheard; they felt like Embassy officials in Moscow, walking in the parks to escape ubiquitous bugs in their offices. Where could they go? In the house the police were everywhere. They could hardly go for a walk without attracting comment. If they went into the garden, even, what would people think—that slimy bastard Fawcett from next door, for example—at the sight of the two of them strolling up and down the path in low, urgent conversation?

In the end it was eleven o'clock, when the police infestation of the house had somewhat abated, before the pair of them, obeying a silent signal from Gordon, could disappear to the bedroom and begin to thrash the matter out.

'If you could talk French,' said Brian, 'we wouldn't have this difficulty.'

'Cut it out. If I could talk French so could your common-or-garden policeman. And what the hell would he think if we started jabbering away in Frog? Come to that, I didn't notice you were so bloody fluent when we were in Tunisia. You never wanted to translate, I remember.'

Tunisia.

'Anyway,' continued Gordon, 'there's no problem now. Any copper comes up those stairs and they'll creak to high heaven. This house was jerry-built before we were born and it's housed Lill for twenty-five years or more. That would wreck the Tower of London. You can hear every goddam thing everybody does.'

'We don't want it to look as if we were conspiring, getting our stories right,' said Brian obstinately.

Gordon sat forward in the little bedroom chair, shoulders hunched, intense, blazing: 'For God's sake, what is this? We're not guilty, remember? Why the hell should we get our stories right? All we have to do is to say to the police what we were going to say . . . tell the truth.'

'Which?' said Brian, still with a mulish expression on his face. He stood by the little fireplace in the bedroom, boarded, up, and with a pathetic little electric fire set in the boards, a useless crusader against the mists and damps of winter. He looked down at it, the long straight lock of hair coming forward as usual over his eyes and making him look even younger and more defenceless than he was.

'Look,' he said: 'we plotted. We intended to do it. We wouldn't want that known. Right?'

'Of course we wouldn't want that known. Why the hell should it be? There's only you and me know.'

'All I'm saying is, we've something to hide. For example, you must have been in the bog in that pub timing yourself for hours, I'd imagine.'

'Didn't you notice I'd gone, then?'

'No. To tell you the truth I forgot all about it.'

'My God, what a partner you make,' groaned Gordon in disgust. 'Well, I was there thirteen minutes. You don't say anything about that, natch.'

'All right, then. But you see what I mean. I *feel* guilty. It doesn't matter that we didn't do it. Morally it's the same.'

'You've got too much bloody imagination. And what's all this about morality? If I plan a murder again I'll get a partner who's all solid muscle and a head six inches thick. You do bugger all, and then you get eaten up with guilt. Forget it, for Chrissake. For all we've done to the contrary, Lill would still be alive now.'

'Just,' said Brian.

'Well, don't you forget it. That policeman's going to be giving you the once-over. I don't want you blubbering and saying "we planned it, Mr Grouser, sir; we're morally guilty." Remember: we've done *nothing,* boyo.'

'OK. But somebody did. Somebody got in first. Don't you even want to know who it was?'

'Some day I might. As of now I just want to get through the next few days. Devoted son mourning his much-loved Mum. After that, I might like to find out.

If it was some mugger I'd like to bash his face in. Doing me out of my fun.'

Brian flinched, then left the mantelpiece and came over to him. 'Some mugger—OK, that will be all very convenient. But what if it was our Debbie? Or old Fred?'

Gordon let out the beginnings of a raucous laugh, then arched his body forward and choked it in his lap.

'Our Fred! He couldn't chop a worm in half with his spade without botching the job.'

'Debbie, then. She hated Lill's guts. More than us.'

'If she did it, she's acting in a damnfool way this morning. Asking about the funeral, and all that!'

'Debbie's like that. She can't hide anything.'

'Well, she'd better start learning, if she's going to go around knocking people off. She'll find herself in some bloody reformatory with a matron the spit image of Lill.'

'Look, face up to it, Gord. What are we going to say? Are we going to put on the grief-stricken act, or are we going to be honest about her?'

'Oh, for God's sake, of course we're not going to be honest about her. Do you think people ever are when there's been a murder? Do they all troop along to the Station and say "I hated her guts, I admit, but I didn't do it"? We're the devoted sons. Everybody thinks so. Lill thought so. We're broken-hearted, like old Fred: all we want is for them to catch the bastard who did it.'

'OK. All I'm saying is there's some pretence.'

'The *same* pretence we've been going on with for years.'

'Debbie knows we hated her.'

'Telepathy, that's all. She couldn't swear to it. Why would she want to? If she knew who'd done it, she'd be all over him like a rash in pure gratitude.'

'If she didn't do it herself.'

'Well, if she did she'll have to look after herself. We've got enough to do worrying about us.'

'You see? It's not that simple. You're starting to act guilty yourself.'

Gordon glowered at him, and banged out of the room. As he ran down the stairs a policeman in the hall looked up at him, curious, speculating.

Down at the Todmarsh Station, Chief Inspector Mc-Hale—sleek and complacent in his recent promotion, a new honour which, like most other things that had ever happened to him, had gone straight to his head—unbent sufficiently to talk over the case with the local man. Haggart was older, wiser, but unused to cases of murder and inclined for that reason to defer without cause. McHale had wandered distantly among the local men drinking their coffee and stuffing thick sandwiches, but now he had come to rest by the window, gazing contemptuously at the little patch of garden worked by the Todmarsh force in their spare time, with its neatly marshalled beds and paths, lawful and orderly. He pursed his lips at the dirty window, and paid little attention to the lower ranks.

'How did the family impress you?' Haggart asked.

'Pretty ordinary collection,' returned McHale, without pausing for thought. 'Cut up, as you'd expect, and saying some silly things, just like everybody does at this sort of time. Perfectly run-of-the-mill lot. Nothing out of the way there.'

'The second boy's at Grammar School, going on to

the University, they say,' said Haggart. McHale merely raised his eyebrows and continued staring out of the window. 'You're not inclined to suspect one of them, then?'

'Not unless I get any evidence that points in that direction,' said McHale confidently. 'You told me this morning they were thought of as a pretty devoted little family. Why should I suspect them?'

Haggart shook his head. 'No obvious reason. Still, I had the impression there was *something*. The mother —the dead woman—had a bit of a reputation.'

'Really? Well, no doubt I'll be learning plenty about *that* in the next few days. What sort of reputation?'

'She was rough. The loud, vulgar type—irritated most people . . .'

'Shouldn't have thought the family were sensitive plants,' said McHale with a superior smile.

'I think she'd slept around a bit in her time—without the husband being aware.'

'I suppose that sort of thing makes a bit of a stir in a small town,' said McHale, still oozing city complacency. 'Well, I'll keep it in mind. No doubt this *could* be a straightforward family killing. On the other hand, it could be a simple robbery with the killing thrown in for kicks. You've no idea how much of that there is these days—and the devil's own job it is to pin it on anyone. Then again, as you yourself said, she wasn't liked.'

'Most folk around here couldn't stand her guts. She touched a nerve, you might say.'

'I know the type, believe me. I expect the family will be able to help us there—who particularly disliked her, and so on.'

'If they know. In a way they'd be the last to hear. I don't suppose Lill—Mrs Hodsden—realized herself. She sort of sailed through life, if you know what I mean. Full of herself, she was, and never gave a damn about what anyone else said or thought. If anyone gave her a piece of their mind, it would be like water off a duck's back.'

'It would get through to the family, though,' said McHale, with his usual congenital confidence. 'Children at school, and all that. I've no doubt they know just who had reason to loathe the mother. I expect when I come to talk to them I'll get a great deal out of that family.'

A sergeant spoke up from the back of the room, undaunted by McHale's air of remote authority, like royalty visiting the other ranks' canteen:

'Those two boys were up to something, up in their bedroom. Chattering away like magpies. One of them started to laugh, and then choked it down. I heard them from the hall.'

Chief Inspector McHale turned and looked at him for a moment, and then said: 'When you're a little older, Sergeant, you'll know that people behave in a funny way when there's a death. They don't tiptoe round and talk in hushed whispers as they're supposed to. And a murder's no different—worse, in fact. There's a lot of tension there, waiting to be released.'

The sergeant's mouth had set firm at the snub. Haggart rushed in to cover over: 'So you don't think of the Hodsdens as murderers, then?'

'In my experience,' said McHale, 'the first things a murderer needs are brains and guts. I wouldn't have said any of the Hodsdens had either in sufficient quantities.'

And nodding in a positively lordly manner, he left the recreation room to take up the threads of the investigation. No one in the room was to know that this was his first proper murder investigation, and indeed he himself had managed to put that fact totally out of his mind.

CHAPTER 9

OLD FRED

When all is said and done, thought Fred, painstakingly buttoning the cuffs of his shirt, being interviewed by the police was a bit of excitement. The whole thing was terribly upsetting, quite horrible, and yet—a sensation of heat in his bowels made him aware that he was thrilled at being at the centre of a real-life sensation. He put on his shabby old grey suit and looked out at the police car by the side of the road outside. It was there to take him to the Station. He caught sight of himself in the bedroom mirror and was shocked to see something like a smile on his lips. He composed his face into an expression of extreme depression. Grief was beyond him, outside his emotional range. He thought: Poor old Lill; she'd have enjoyed all the fuss. She always liked a bit of life.

Thought is perhaps too definite a word for what went on in Fred's head: impressions, feelings, vague impulses and desires floated through his brain like skeletal autumn leaves, driven by the vaguest breeze, slow, wanton, uncatchable. Fred could never have verbalized one of these thoughts, still less could he have argued for any of his opinions. Still, there was this low heat in his belly, this smouldering excitement, that made him, today, more than usually self-conscious, awake to everything going on around him. In the road outside a police constable got out of the car and leaned heavily over the top of it, looking towards the house. They're waiting for me, thought Fred. He straightened his tie, dusted a speck of dirt from a sleeve, then walked round the double bed and left the front bedroom he had shared for nearly thirty years with Lill.

In the car Fred was silent. What was appropriate conversation for a man whose wife had just been garrotted in a public thoroughfare to make with the policeman who is driving him to the police station for questioning? Fred's was not an inventive mind. As he got into the car he hazarded a 'Looks like rain, don't it?' but thenceforth he held his peace; blew, in fact, on those little coals of excitement in his guts. He was head of the household, going—the *first* to go —to talk to the man investigating the murder of his wife. Made you think.

Awkwardness made him shuffle when he was led into the presence of McHale, but then he told himself that that was stupid, and took his eyes from the brown lino on the floor. The sight of McHale, poised elegantly and impressively over an unnaturally tidy desk, confirmed Fred's impressions of earlier in the day. Good-looking chap. Good class of chap, too. Well spoken, clean, a natural leader. Ambitious, capable. Fred respected that kind of chap. Voted for them— the Conservatives—in local elections. You could trust a chap like that to get things done.

He said: 'You've got to get him, that bastard. Must have been some kind of crazy mugger, eh? Christ, you wonder what the country's coming to in this day and age, don't you? Bombs, assassinations, and now this.'

McHale, though he was not inclined to see Lill's murder in a national context, did in general terms agree with Fred: the murderer was probably some stray maniac. Last year there had been, in the Cumbledon area, that nasty business of the gay ripper. He had not, as it happened, got very far—being so unlucky as to choose for his second rip a fair-haired, angelic-looking judo black belt. But the case had impressed McHale (who had not been on it) with a sense of meaningless, perverse horror. It had confirmed, for no very obvious reasons, some odd feelings he had about the moral health of the nation. The garrotting of Lill Hodsden seemed to him to bear the same hallmarks. But of course, as he told himself, his mind was very much open.

He said: 'You may well be right. And believe me, I've got a whole troop of people working on those lines—' As if to confirm what he said the telephone now rang. He snapped a couple of 'yes's and a 'no' into the mouthpiece and then slammed it down. 'But of course,' he went on, 'until we can be sure we've got to fill in the picture as far as your wife is concerned—just as a matter of routine. I'm sure you understand that.'

'Oh aye,' said Fred.

I hope you do, thought McHale. He took hold of a handbag that was lying on his desk, a plastic affair that made only the most half-hearted attempt to imagine itself leather. Its red-brown colour was clearly designed to tone in with Lill's hair. At the sight of it in McHale's hands, two little tears squeezed themselves out of the corners of Fred's eyes, and ambled down his cheeks. He wiped them off with an earthy handkerchief.

'Sorry,' he said: 'brought her back to me, like.'

'Quite natural,' said McHale briskly.

Fred—hesitantly, as if expecting to hear the upbraiding voice of Lill asking him what he thought he was doing—took the bag in his work-rasped hands and began to rummage inexpertly around in it.

'Can you spot anything missing?' asked McHale unhopefully.

'There's nowt as far as I can see,' said Fred. 'But then I wouldn't really know. I've never been one to go poking around in my wife's things.'

'No, of course not,' said McHale. 'But you would know if she'd been accustomed to carry anything valuable around with her?'

'Can't say she had anything valuable,' said Fred. 'We're plain folks, like I said. 'Course, there was the engagement ring . . .' Thirty-five bob, he remembered, back in Festival of Britain year, bought with a modest treble-chance win that had also run to a plaice and chips lunch at the Odeon cafeteria. He'd been happy that day. He did not see the sneer on the face of McHale. McHale had seen the ring too.

'No—the ring was still on the—she was still wearing it,' he said. 'And your son said she wouldn't have been carrying much money . . .'

'Don't know what *he'd* know about it,' grumbled Fred, as if loath to share the limelight. 'We wouldn't know, would we? She might have had money from anywhere.'

'Really?' McHale jumped in, leaned imposingly forward and looked Fred in the eyes. 'You think she could have had money you know nothing about?'

Fred jumped. That was coming it rather fast.

'I didn't question her about money,' he said, his mouth set in an obstinate line. 'Just gave her the housekeeping and let her get on with it.' (The housekeeping, be it said, was all but a quid or so of Fred's weekly wage.)

'But you think she could have got money from somewhere else?'

'Could have,' said Fred, still mulish.

'Where, for example?'

'How would I know? I tell you, I didn't ask questions.'

'But it was you who made the suggestion, Mr Hodsden.'

'I didn't make any suggestions at all. All I'm saying is, with Lill you never knew. She was a smart one, was Lill.'

McHale was bewildered. He was not sure how carefully he needed to tread. How besottedly stupid was Fred Hodsden? Or was he a complaisant husband? He dipped a toe in the water.

'Your wife had been out visiting, hadn't she? At a Mr . . . Hamilton Corby's.'

Fred, it seemed, regarded this as a change of subject, and shifted in his chair so he did not have to see the red-brown handbag. 'That's right. Well, Mrs Corby really, of course. She's an invalid. She'd been very good to her, my Lill had. Visited her twice a week, regular as clockwork. She'll miss Lill will Mrs Corby, poor soul.'

MsHale raised, fractionally, a silver-blond eyebrow at the cretinous obtuseness of mankind. From a glance at Lill's dead body he could have told that she was no devoted sick-room visitor. 'Would there be any reason' he asked, treading warily over Fred's stupidity like a super-power edging its way into a Third World country, 'why Mr Corby should have paid her a sum of money last night?'

Fred looked at him blankly: 'No, not as I know of . . . Mind you, he was a generous man: found a place for our Gordon when he came out of the army, even though work's scarce in the yards. But what would he give her money for?'

'Or jewellery, perhaps? A present of jewellery?'

At last the idea got through to Fred. He struggled forward in his chair, spluttering and coughing. 'Here, what do you mean? What are you trying to say? Ruddy cheek! There's no one can say my Lill was one of that sort!'

'You misunderstand me,' said McHale with a patient smile. 'I merely meant he might have given her something, some token, as a thank-you . . . for her care of his wife . . . Perhaps some trinket of his wife's that she had no more use for—after all, I gather that she's bedridden.'

Fred sank back into his chair, apparently somewhat mollified. 'Oh well, if that was all you were implying, that's all right. I suppose he might have. But it hadn't happened before not to my knowledge.'

'You took me up very sharp there, Mr Hodsden,' said McHale, super-smooth, in a way that made Fred sweat. 'Is there something you're keeping back? About your wife's relationships with other men, for example? Did she have—friendships?'

Fred, having once exploded, seemed now to be working on a longer fuse. 'She was a real character, my Lill. Everybody knew her in this town. She was everyone's friend. Brightened up the place as soon as she came here. Ask anyone. Ask 'em at the Rose and Crown. 'Course she had friendships.'

'With men?'

'Men and women. And I expect there's dirty-minded people round the town who might have talked about it. I don't mean you—you're paid to snoop. But people do talk. Any road, they'd've been wrong. Lill wasn't like that. She was just—outgoing. But at heart she was a family person . . . She was a wonderful mother.'

A memory of the Hodsden daughter, her eye bruised, wafted through McHale's mind. He lowered his head and made a little note on his writing-pad.

'Of course, I'll be talking to your family,' he said. 'And then there are the friends you mention. Who would you say were your wife's greatest friends?'

Fred drew a finger round the collar that loosely spanned his scraggy, contracting neck. 'Well,' he said, 'there's Mrs Fawcett next door, but I wouldn't say she was a particular . . . And then there's Mrs Corby, of course; they were devoted . . . But I'm out all day, so I . . .'

'I see,' said McHale. 'Well, I'll ask your daughter. I expect she's more likely to know.'

He preened himself on his sharpness when he saw Fred's reaction. His concrete-grey face went rose-pink, and again he bent forward, choking: 'Well, Debbie's away all day too, you know, at school,' he said and then it seemed to strike him that anything he said might make things worse and he trailed off into silence.

'Still, women talk to their daughters, don't they?'

said McHale, in his most molasses voice. 'Or is it
more your sons your wife was close to? I seem to have
heard . . .'

'Oh aye,' said Fred, leaning back in his chair with
relief and now seeming to have no jealousy of sharing
the spotlight with his sons: 'Gordon and Brian wor-
shipped the ground she walked on. Couldn't do
enough for her. Yes, you talk to Gordon and Brian.'

'Mr Hodsden,' said McHale, again leaning forward
and looking impressive, 'there is one thing I have to
ask you: where were you and the rest of the family
last night?'

' 'Course you have to ask it: I understand. It's easy,
anyway. Debbie and I were both home, and Brian
and Gordon were down the Rose and Crown.'

'I see. So you and—Debbie, is it?—can vouch for each
other, can you?'

'Oh aye. She was in her room and I was watching
telly.'

'Well, that's not quite vouching for each other, as
we understand it. Did you see much of each other
during the evening—she came down now and then,
I suppose?'

'No, no—she didn't come down.'

'Not once?'

'No—but I know she was up there . . .' Fred pulled
himself together, backing away from the brink of
telling how he knew Debbie was up in her room, and
finished lamely: 'I'd've heard if she'd come down or
gone out.'

'But you might have nodded off. People do.'

'Oh no. No. Lill was very . . .' Again he pulled
himself up and shook himself, as if bewildered by

the web of deception he was entangling himself in. 'Lill didn't like me falling asleep. Said it was dangerous, 'specially if I had my pipe in. No, I definitely didn't fall asleep.'

'I see. But that means nobody can vouch for you, I suppose. Nobody came to the door, or anything?'

'No—not as I mind. It's all become a bit of a blur, like, after hearing about . . . it. Still, it doesn't do to give way, does it? Life's got to go on, and there's the family to see to.' Fred seemed suddenly to become conscious that he was rambling into matters irrelevant to the police investigation, and asked: 'Was there anything more?'

'No, nothing for the moment, I think. Of course, the police will be around your place quite a lot in the future, I'm afraid. So if there's anything else crops up I want to ask about, I can contact you there.'

'Yes, I see,' said Fred. 'Well, we all want to help you, you can bank on that. The main thing is, you catch the bugger who done it.' He got up and shambled to the door, but once he hesitated, as if thinking hard. Then he turned and said: 'Still, you want to be careful what you say about my Lill and other men. That's libel, that is. You ought to watch your tongue!'

'Mr Hodsden, I was implying nothing—'

'Well, you ought to watch it. I nearly fetched you one then, I did!'

As Fred Hodsden fumbled his way out of the room, McHale smiled a thin smile like winter sunshine on Northern waters. He did not see Fred Hodsden as a murderer. In fact, he held to his opinion that none of the Hodsdens looked like murderers. Still, there might be some amusement to be got out of them on the way.

Dominic McHale was born and brought up near Bristol. His family was doubtless Scottish from way back, but there was nothing of the border ruffian or the highland savage left in their blood. They had obviously been respectable for centuries. His father was a tax official, and one who brought a good deal of cold enthusiasm to his job. His mother was local president of the Mothers' Union, and wonderful at organizing bazaars. Dominic had been a superior child: at school he was good at games and held his own in academic subjects, but he was aloof, and less than popular. The High School girls went with boys who were less good-looking but more forthcoming. He was sure he would get into Oxford, and he very nearly did: he was on the borderline, but in the end the commoner's place went to a boy from a Northern comprehensive, to make the intake tables look more respectable. 'If my father had been a bloody miner I'd have got in,' he remarked bitterly to his contemporaries. A tax-inspector father was neither fish nor fowl as far as admissions committees were concerned, and could never swing a vote in his favour.

He did not settle for red-brick, or white tile, or plate glass. People so sure of themselves never settle for anything less than their deserts. The only thing that could salve his pride was a complete change of course. He went into the police force. When all was said and done, people in general always felt at a disadvantage when dealing with a policeman. Even a little afraid . . .

He thought, too, that his (as he saw it) cool, ra-

tional mind would make him a cinch for promotion
in the Detective branch—even for mild local fame. At
last—distinctly more slowly than he had expected—
the promotion had come. He was now a Chief Inspector. He had also a cool wife with two well-drilled
children in a tasteful home in a nice suburb of Cumbledon. He had arrived. Until the next move upwards.

He strolled confidently into the outer office, a hive
of activity, with junior personnel rushing hither and
thither in the excitement of the first murder in Todmarsh's living memory. McHale said to Inspector
Haggart, who was standing by the desk, 'Send someone
up for the elder Hodsden boy, would you?' and then
seemed inclined to linger.

'Didn't get much out of Fred Hodsden, I reckon,'
said Inspector Haggart, when he had made all the
necessary arrangements.

'Hmmm—so-so,' said McHale. 'Not the brightest of
intellects. Not the strongest of bodies either: can't see
him strangling a fit, hulking woman like that one in
there.' He jerked his thumb in the direction of the
morgue and Lill's body (white topped with claret
red, like some hideous Andy Warhol woman).

The Inspector looked dubious: 'You can't tell with
these skinny, wiry types. I've known farm labourers
you'd think the first March winds'd blow away, but
you get in their way in a pub brawl and you wonder
what hit you.'

'Hmmm,' said McHale.

'Was he at home last night?'

'So he says. Him and the daughter.'

'They certainly were when the police arrived. But
it's funny—'

'What is?' McHale raised those bored, superior eyebrows.

'Jim—that's Partridge, the constable that got there first. He—oh, there he is: he can tell you himself. Jim! Tell the Inspector what you told me—about what happened when you got to the Hodsdens' last night.'

Jim Partridge had ambled over, a big, slow Devonshire man. 'Aye, that were odd,' he said. 'I told him—gentle, like—what had happened and he were, well, you'd say he were overcome. I'd swear it were genuine. And then, he pulled himself together like, and instead of calling to his daughter upstairs, he went up to her. And it's funny, but I thought I heard a key turn in the lock. Then he told her, and she came down.'

'Ah!' said McHale. And then, with that condescending smile that robbed his compliments of any warmth, he said: 'Good observation, Partridge!'

CHAPTER 10

HALF TRUTHS

Fred arrived back home in an uncertain mood. He was unsure whether the interview had been a success or not, whether he had imposed his importance, as husband of the deceased, on the mind of the rather distant young Chief Inspector from Cumbledon. It was a question, as even Fred realized, whether he had been impressive or ridiculous. And then there were those questions about Debbie . . . He did not feel he had shone there. If only Lill were still around to tell him what to do.

He came through the kitchen and hall and into the front room, and immediately blinked in bewilderment. Something was different; something was wrong. He sensed it immediately. Gordon and Brian were there: Brian reading in the easy chair by the window, Gordon standing by the fireplace exuding caged energy. He was smoking—he'd taken it up again. But still, something else was different. Fred blinked again, and looked around.

'How did it go?' asked Gordon. 'What's the bloke like? What did he ask you?'

'Here,' said Fred, his voice rising in pitch to a tone of feeble bluster. 'What've you been doing? There's something wrong here. Where are them ornaments of Lill's?'

He'd got it. The room was different: it had been denuded. Lill had prided herself on her bits and pieces. The little brass knick-knacks on the mantel-piece—a bell, a yacht, a tiny candlestick of vaguely Jewish design. The flower stand, silvered plastic, de-picting a reclining Venus, which always sat on the television. The souvenir novelties from Blackpool, Southsea and Torquay. All the vases from Tunisia, bought from the beach vendors around Hammamet. They had festered over every surface, becoming more huddled together as their numbers had grown. Once a week Lill had flipped a duster lovingly in their di-rection. They were her pride, and each one had a story attached to it, to be told to the occasional visitor to the front room. Now many were missing: hardly more than half were there, newly distributed around. The room had indefinably become less Lill. That's what was annoying Fred.

'What've you done with her bits and pieces?' he repeated.

'We sort of sorted them out,' said Brian.

'Well, what do you mean by it? What've you done with them?'

'We put them away—just some of them. None of us would want to dust that lot.'

'Putting her things away the day after she dies! I never heard the like.'

'We had to,' said Gordon, his voice deep with emo-tion. 'They reminded us of Mum. It was too—poig-nant.'

Fred looked at him. That was a funny word for Gordon to use. Fred wasn't sure what to make of it.

Anyone might think Gordon wasn't serious. He felt uncertain, frustrated. Now it was the boys who were bewildering him; yesterday it had been Debbie.

'Well, put 'em out and put 'em back where they should be,' he muttered. 'You don't know what people might think . . . Any road, Lill'd hate to think of them mouldering away in some drawer.'

He bumbled along querulously to his chair, fished out his tin of tobacco and began rolling himself a scraggy cigarette, dropping strands of tobacco into his lap from his shaking hands.

'Well, how did it go?' repeated Gordon, apparently unperturbed. 'What did you tell him?'

'Told him everything I know, of course,' said Fred, still dimly bellicose. 'We've got to help the police as much as we can . . . naturally.'

'Did you tell him about Mum and Debbie?' asked Brian.

' 'Course I didn't. What business is it of theirs? It's got nowt to do with it. Just a little family squabble. So don't you two go telling him neither.'

'So you didn't tell him all you know,' said Brian.

'None of your smartyboots remarks. I told him everything he needed to know. Just because for once in their lives your mum and Debbie fell out . . .'

For once in their lives! Brian put aside his book and looked at Fred in wonder. Talk about pity my simplicity! Was Fred completely stupid, or did he just genuinely fail to notice things? Debbie and Lill had disliked each other, it seemed, all Debbie's short life: open warfare had been declared when Debbie was twelve. That was the occasion when Lill, in one superbly timed swoop of her brawny arms, had shoved her daughter's head into the plate of cornflakes she was supposed to be eating. Since then life at the Hodsdens had been punctuated by such incidents: Debbie's first fashionable shoes thrown into the kitchen stove; her first lipstick ground under Lill's heel into the rose-bed; Debbie herself pulled upstairs by her hair after some piece of cheek. Culminating in that fight in the kitchen and the damaging bruise seen by everybody on the school bus, by all the girls and mistresses at school.

As if reading his brother's thoughts, Gordon turned to Fred and said: 'It's not us you have to tell to keep quiet. It's Debbie. We're not ones to wash the family's dirty linen in public, but she wouldn't care tuppence who she told.'

'She's not that daft,' said Fred, totally without conviction. 'Why should she go blabbing?'

'To get attention. She's that age.'

'And have them on her back, thinking she done it?'

'She's got a perfect alibi, remember. She was locked in upstairs and you were down here on guard. She's only got to tell them that and they'll see she couldn't have done it.'

'I might have dropped off,' said Fred reluctantly, looking down at his knees in embarrassment. 'I don't say I did, mind.'

'There's still the locked door. I bet you didn't tell the Chief Inspector about that, either.'

'Well, how could I, when I didn't tell him about the other?' Fred grumbled his way into silence and digested the points that had been made. He said at last: 'Well, one of you'd better talk to our Debbie. Make her see sense. Keep her mouth shut. We don't want to get ourselves talked about.'

It seemed a curious hope after a murder in the

family. But Brian's attention was focused on something else he'd said.

'Why one of us? Why not you?'

'Eh,' said Fred uneasily. 'I've never had that much to say to Debbie. You two are more her own age. She'll take it better coming from you.'

Gordon and Brian looked at each other. But at that moment a constable appeared at the sitting-room door and asked Gordon to come with him to the Station. As he straightened up and walked lightly from the room with his impressive athlete's walk, Fred turned to Brian with a new access of confidence and said: 'It'll have to be you then, as talks to her.' He got up and marched from the room, turning at the door to say:

'And put them ornaments back, double quick!'

Goldon, squatting on the hard kitchen chair opposite McHale's desk, his dark wavy head in his large workingman's hands, said: 'She was a wonderful person. We loved her. There was nobody like her. 'Course, old Fred—Dad—does his best, but she was head of the family. She had so much personality.' He straightened up, and swallowed. 'Everything's so different, now she's gone. The world's a different place.'

(Am I overdoing it? I've got to get the message across, but enough is enough. He'll think I'm a right softie. Brian thought he wasn't too bright. Hope he's right about that. Don't like the type myself. We had officers like that in the army. One of them damn near led us into an IRA boobytrap. Perhaps that's what Brian means.)

'Sorry about that,' he said more normally. 'Haven't

really got over the shock yet. Somehow it all seemed to happen in such a rush.'

McHale showed standard sympathy. 'Perfectly natural. You and your brother were at the pub, is that right? You heard down there?'

'That's it. That made it worse. All that singing, all those people. And we were a bit high: there was a celebration on—bachelor party, you know what they're like. What a time to hear your mother's been done in!'

'Yes, I can understand that. I suppose you were there all evening, were you?'

'That's right. From about eight till . . . till Jack Perkins came over and brought it out.'

'Then there'll be no difficulty in getting people to vouch for you, I imagine. You didn't leave the party at all?'

'No. I went to the . . . toilet, I expect. Yes, I must have. I was drinking beer. Otherwise I was around all the time. Having a great time. Makes you think.'

'Now, before yesterday evening, in the last few days, for example, was there anything—in the family, say, or in your mother's relationships with . . . friends —that had stood out, been in any way unusual?'

Gordon seemed to have a big think. 'Not that I can remember. She did all the things she usually did. She had a pretty fixed programme: had to, because she was a busy woman. Like she always went to the Corbys' on Mondays and Thursdays.'

(I can see it all: middle-aged body to middle-aged body in unlovely huddles on the sofa, bulges bouncing for a few minutes, and then Lill screwing out of him what she wanted: the odd quid here, the second-hand car there. I can just picture it.)

'Ah yes. That was to see—to visit the sick lady, Mrs Corby, was it not?'

Gordon made a quick decision.

'Well, six of one and half a dozen of the other, I expect. Old Hamilton C. admired her, I can tell you that. He's got an eye for a good-looking woman. Men who marry for money usually have. No harm in it, of course. For Mum it was just a bit of excitement. We're not living in the nineteenth century, after all.' He looked at Inspector McHale with a roguish glance of male conspiracy. 'You're a man of the world.'

McHale responded with a similar glance, the small change of pub and police canteen, and sank back in his chair. 'Very sensible of you to tell me. And what about your father?'

'Old Fr—Dad? He didn't know, naturally not. He's not that bright, as you may have noticed.' Gordon was now relaxed in his chair, sure he had done the right thing. 'But don't get me wrong. I'm not saying there was anything—anything really going on.'

'I see . . .'

'Not anything serious. It just gave a bit of spice to Mum's life. After all, you've seen Dad. He's no big pools win. He looks years older than Mum did, and sort of feeble, to put it bluntly. And Mum was still a woman in her prime.'

(How does it look, that corpse in its prime, now lying probably in some police morgue here or in Cumbledon? The red hair with the line of brown roots, the flesh—white, waxy and transparent now, like when I identified that soldier in Londonderry, when they wouldn't let me see more than his head and shoulders. She's as lifeless as him now, more lifeless than a Tussaud waxwork, Lill who made me what I am.)

'So you think, anyway, there was more to your mother's visits to the Corbys' than holding the invalid's hands?' said McHale with a pale smile.

'Natch. I expect she gave Hamilton C. a bit of womanly sympathy after she'd been up with Mrs Corby. Poisonous woman that, everyone says. She's hardly been seen by mortal eye for five years or more, other than poor old Hamilton's. He doesn't have much of a life when you think about it, poor old bugger. He's been good to me too, in his way—got me a job at the shipyard, and that.'

'Do you think your mother had other—friendships like that?'

'Oh, I expect so. I've been away, in the army, so I wouldn't know any of the details. But a woman like that's bound to attract men friends, I'd say.'

'I expect you're right,' said McHale smoothly. 'Now, you don't think there'd been anything else of interest—anything unusual happening in your mother's life in the last few days? For example, in the family . . . ?'

Gordon took another quick decision. 'Oh no. We jog along pretty much as usual most of the time. I mean, nothing out of the ordinary happens. Fred—Dad—goes to work in the park, or the Memorial Gardens. Bri goes to school—he'll be going to university next year. I work in the shipyard, do a bit of training some evenings. Debbie's still at school. We go to the pub of an evening now and then, mostly Saturdays. That's the usual pattern.'

'So there hadn't been any disturbances in the past week or so? Any . . . rows, for example?'

'No,' said Gordon. 'We're not much of a family for rows. Mum kept things on an even keel, mostly. And if anything else unusual had happened, we'd all have heard of it, that's for sure. Mum wasn't one to keep things back.'

(It can't do any harm, not telling him. No good Brian priming Debbie to hold her tongue and me blabbing it out. Stick to one plan. Then if it comes out, as it probably will, it will just look like the devoted family sticking together. It won't look *suspicious*. Christ! The idea of Lill the Peacemaker, though!)

'I'm wondering—' said McHale cautiously—'I'm trying to get an idea of what sort of woman your mother was. Do you think you could try to sum her up for me?'

(Careful: those cold blue eyes, watching me. Don't make the mistake of overdoing it. None of the ham stuff. Only pull out some of the stops.)

'I suppose everyone thinks their Mum is something special, don't they?' said Gordon slowly. 'Anyway, all I can say is, ours was to us. She was a very warm person, very vital. She was so outgoing you always felt it when she was around. The rest of us don't amount to much. But everybody in Todmarsh knew Mum. She'll really be missed around here!'

(A slut, a loud-mouthed, vulgar slut who ruined my life.)

When Gordon had been thanked, and the wintry eyes had simulated understanding and sympathy, he was shown out. In the outer office he told the constable who had driven him down that he preferred to walk home. As he made his way along, very slow, hunched over (with grief, for all anybody knew), he went over in his mind the interview with McHale. On the whole he felt he had got things right. Fred

had been established as feeble and foolish, he himself—and the rest of the children—as besottedly devoted. Any suspicion there might be about people in
Lill's personal life had been directed outwards: at
Wilf Hamilton Corby. Even at his wife. And they
were rich bastards who could look after themselves.
Any road, he'd done his best. The only possible problem was Debbie. Well, if she wanted to muck things
up, that was her affair. She wasn't a girl to listen to
reason, and she'd have to bear the consequences. In
any case, nobody could seriously suspect a sixteen-
year-old girl of killing her own mother. Could they?

Brian, heavy-handed, heavy-hearted, took Lill's knick-
knacks one by one from the back of the sideboard
and began to restore them to their rightful, Lill-or-
dained places. The little brass windmill, the plaster
duck with the cheeky expression, the model of Anne
Hathaway's cottage. And all the pots and plates from
Tunisia, with their sharp, pressing associations—the
sun, the leafy gardens around the hotel, with their
orange and lemon trees, and the loose-bowelled birds
overhead; the endless beach, with Lill in her two-
piece holding court, surrounded by sellers of rugs
and sun-hats, toy camels and earthenware pots, sitting
at her feet, dark, doe-eyed and teasing, delighting
in the polyglot sparring before bounding off to more
profitable prey: the German couples, pumped full of
heavy food and deutschmarks. And Lill, lying back
on the beach, holding her nasty little vase or plate
and announcing which of the vendors she fancied.
    Brian looked around the room. Now everything
was back, down to the dreariest little pot, the price
Lill willingly paid for five more minutes' attention.

The room had returned to normal, Lill had resumed her sway. Brian felt he had been appointed keeper of the Lill Hodsden Memorial Museum. To put the thought out of his mind he went up to talk to Debbie.

Debbie had mostly kept to her room since Lill's death—almost as if she were still locked in. As if to emphasize, in fact, that she *had* been locked in, and no one had lifted a finger to help her. Or perhaps she did not care to mingle with the family and join in their grief, real or pretended. At any rate, she was not going to be hypocritical: she was not grief-stricken and she was not ashamed. She kept insisting on this to herself. She lay on her bed, exaggeratedly casual, reading a Harold Robbins.

'Hello, Debbie.'

'Hello.' Debbie went on leafing through her block-buster from double-cross to rape, exaggeratedly calm, taking no notice of her brother. Her dark brown hair fell down untidily over her sharp, passionate face. One day Debbie would be a beauty; even now she was the sort of schoolgirl one noticed, wondered about. She turned another page, and cupped her chin in her hands. Brian knew perfectly well she was not reading.

'About the police . . .' he began.

She looked up. 'Dishy, wasn't he?' she said.

'I thought he looked rather stupid,' said Brian, allowing himself to be sidetracked.

'That too,' said Debbie.

'But about when he talks to you: we thought—'

'Oh yes? Have you been concerning yourselves with me down there? That's nice. That's heart-warming.'

'—we thought it would be best if you didn't mention that little trouble between you and Mum.'

'Little trouble? You mean when she half knocked my block off?'

'Well, all the more reason for not mentioning it.'

'I don't know what it's got to do with you lot, but if the copper doesn't bring it up, I won't.'

'But if he does—'

'Well, I'll tell him, of course. Why not? I've got nothing to lose.'

'I wouldn't be too sure of that. The Inspector seems to think it was some kind of mugger, but if he hears there'd been trouble in the family it'll direct his attention here. And after all, you wouldn't want that.'

'Wouldn't I? Why wouldn't I? Is he supposed to think we were all devoted to her? Well, *I* wasn't.'

'Now, Debbie—'

'Were *you*, Brian? Were *you*?'

Brian swallowed. 'Of course I was. We all were. And all we want is to find out who did it. That's why we don't want to give a false impression.'

'That's what you *do* want to give. If you go round spreading the idea that Lill was loved by all who knew her, they're never going to find out who did it. Perhaps that's what you want, at heart. Well, I'm not going along. If he asks me, I'm going to tell him the truth.'

'You'd be a fool to.'

'Why? I was locked in this room all evening, with Fred on guard downstairs. I couldn't have been more out of it if I'd been in Australia. I'm one person he's not going to suspect.'

Brian went to the window. 'You could have climbed out.'

'Through those bloody roses? I'd've been cut to bits. Look at my hands—see any scratches?' She held out her hands, which were inky rather than bloody. 'I thought of it, actually, and decided against it. If I'd managed to get down, I could never have got back up. Look out: there'd be lots of broken stems and crushed leaves if I'd climbed out and in.'

Brian looked out. The climbing rose clearly hadn't been disturbed. He turned back into the room, disappointed, but as his eye lighted on the door he was struck by a flash of inspiration:

'Of course,' he said. 'The key.' He saw Debbie's eyelids flicker briefly.

'There was no key. Mum locked me in and took it, remember?'

Brian went out on to the landing and grabbed the key to the next room, the double bedroom shared by Lill and Fred. 'This house was jerry-built in the 'thirties. I bet any key turns the lock of any of the doors.' He jiggled it about and then turned it triumphantly. 'See! It does. This place is no Broadmoor.'

'Well, so what? I was in here: I couldn't dart out and get one of the other keys.'

'You had one in here in readiness, I bet. None of us ever locks the bedroom door, so it wouldn't be missed. The last time one of these was locked was—what? two years ago, and then it was you being locked in, just like last night. Mum locked you in because you'd been at her make-up. I bet you've had one of the other keys in here all that time, in case it happened again.'

'Prove it.'

'I bet the police could. By examining the locks and keys. Scratches and that.'

'Are you going along to them to suggest it? You're

the one who's promoting the idea of the idyllically happy Hodsden family, remember. Anyway, if the subject comes up in future, I'll be able to say that if the key of Lill's bedroom has been used in my lock, it's because you just tried it out.' Brian looked down at the key in his hands in dismay. 'You really are the lousiest detective. Now go away and leave me alone.'

'Look, Debbie,' said Brian, coming to sit down on the side of the bed, 'all I'm trying to say is this: your alibi's not foolproof by a long chalk. You'd be a fool to dub yourself in by broadcasting all the family dirt. If you do that you'll do none of us any good. Nor Achituko either, for that matter.'

Debbie blinked again. It was clear she had not thought of Achituko. She thought for a while. 'Well, I suppose I won't say anything. But you needn't think I'm going through with all this disgusting pretence—'

'What pretence?'

'That we were all devoted to Lill. One big happy family, with her the light of all our lives. I bet Gordon's plugging that line down at the Station now. I think it's disgusting.'

'Just so long as you keep quiet about the fight. And about how you didn't get on with her.'

'Didn't get on! What a lovely expression! She made me puke. I loathed the sight of her. And so did you and Gordon. Didn't you, Brian?'

Brian jumped off the bed and headed for the door. But even as he escaped through it she threw out the query to him yet once more: 'Didn't you, Brian?'

And she burst out laughing at his pale, anxious face. Then she put aside her book and lay back to think things through.

CHAPTER 11

BRIAN AND DEBBIE

The two younger Hodsdens, McHale thought to himself later in the day, exhausted by his excursion into the proletariat, were clearly a cut or two above Fred and Gordon in the mental-agility stakes, but he would hardly call them intelligent.

McHale set great store by intelligence in his thinking about the murderer. On the one hand, this killing might be a totally random piece of brutality, in which case the culprit would be difficult to spot because the field was impossibly wide. On the other, it might be a personal thing, a premeditated crime in which Lill Hodsden and Lill alone was the intended victim, and in that case he was convinced that the murderer was a deep one indeed. These two solutions had one thing in common: they demanded great intelligence and insight on the part of the investigating officer. McHale was convinced that he had them; therefore he was convinced this was a crime that demanded them. He was not a man to be content with apprehending common or garden criminals, not he.

So, without the thought consciously surfacing, he was on the look-out for a suitable partner in a duel of brains, and he did not feel he found him in the Hodsden family.

Brian, no doubt, was bright enough as schoolboys went, but he was hardly Oxford material, McHale decided. In addition, there was the undoubted fact that, by any standard of everyday life, Brian was 'wet'. The word belonged to McHale's generation and his attitude of mind, and he stuck it on Brian like a price-tag. The boy looked years younger than he was, had a confident manner which highlighted rather than concealed the fact that he was a bundle of nerves, and seemed to know no more of the world than a day-old chick. Add to that a slight frame and an air of frailness (he somehow did not seem to fit into his jeans and check shirt, and what kind of clothes were they, anyway, for someone who'd just lost their mother?) and McHale felt quite safe in marking him down in his mind as 'feeble', and ruling a line through him on his list of suspects.

Brian's account of the evening before largely confirmed that of his brother.

'Well, it was pretty drunken,' he said, pushing back a lank lock of hair with a gesture that McHale found irritating and pathetic. 'I'm not all that used to these do's, and I was just thinking we ought to be making it home when . . . when . . .' He swallowed. 'Gordon's more the type for that sort of thing: he was the life and soul of the party—had a joke with everyone there.'

'He was in the Rose and Crown the whole evening?'

'Oh yes. I was watching him, because of course I felt a bit strange. They were his friends: he knew everybody and I didn't. He probably had the odd quick trip to the loo, but that was all. Ask anyone.'

'And you?'

'Well, the same, really. I suppose I went to the loo—yes, I did, once. Otherwise I was there in the

Saloon Bar, either talking to someone, or just watching. I expect some of the people there will remember —the more sober ones.'

Like his brother, Brian was sure there had been no ructions in the Hodsden family in the days before the murder. They were not that sort of family. Like his brother, he was willing to admit (not surprisingly, since they had had a hushed, hurried consultation before he was called down to the Station) that his mother might have had the occasional flirtation, with one or other of the men on the fringes of her life, though he justified this in different terms.

'People's life-styles have changed,' he said, with that horribly unconvincing man-of-the-world air. 'Nobody thinks twice about that sort of thing these days.'

Not in Todmarsh? said McHale to himself sceptically. He knew his small-town England and its inhabitants. Permissiveness had not reached them, and if it did they would not know what to do with it. He also noticed Brian's use of the phrase 'life-styles' and thought: pretentious little prig!

Brian's estimate of his mother was less breathlessly admiring than Gordon's (they had agreed that too much of that sort of thing might arouse rather than avert suspicion), but it was equally wholehearted.

'Of course, she wasn't an educated woman at all,' he said. 'Probably you would have called her common.' (It was a shrewd shot. McHale would certainly have called her common, and preened himself on that impeccable, inland revenue background that allowed him to do so. He hardly even bothered to gesture a dissent.) 'But she had more life than a hundred more intelligent people, and she had a wonderful human understanding. Nobody could ever be dull when she was around.' (Thank God, he thought, now I have the right to be dull.) Then he pulled himself up for a suitable summing up of Lill's life and works. 'She was the sort of mother who influences your whole life. She'll always be with me.'

He never spoke a truer word.

Debbie Hodsden was another kettle of fish entirely. In some ways even less mature than Brian, still she seemed to nurse some kind of inner confidence which nourished and protected her. At any rate, it was only rarely that the Chief Inspector dented her breezy front. Unlike Brian, who seemed to have shrunk into his jeans and gone too far, Debbie bloomed out of her school uniform, not so much physically, like a younger version of overblown Lill, but emotionally, as if proclaiming that it represented a stage in her life that in reality was past for ever.

She made no elaborate show of grief for Lill. She appeared serious, sober even, but there was no question (as there had been with Gordon) of her being about to burst into tears. Her notion of the proper behaviour was to be sensible and calm, and leave it at that.

'Mum? What kind of a person? Well, she was very extroverted—big voice, big personality, you know the type. I expect you can guess just by looking at her. I suppose you'd call her common.' (McHale blinked at the repetition. On reflection he decided to feel flattered at being the type of man who inevitably would call Lill Hodsden common.) 'Well—that's what she was, all right. But a lot of people like that.'

'You got on with her all right?'

'Oh yes, we jogged along. Of course, most girls have problems with their mothers—'

'Oh yes?'

'Well, they get jealous of their growing up. It sort of dates them, you know. Makes people think they're past it. So we had a few argie-bargies about my wearing makeup, modern clothes, and that sort of thing.'

'I see. Nothing worse than that?'

'Oh no. Just the normal.'

'You say she resented your growing up. Do you mean she liked to think she was still attractive to men?'

'Well, of course. Naturally. Everyone wants to think they're still attractive to the other sex. I expect you like women to notice you, don't you?' She launched a provocative smile at him.

'We weren't talking—'

'I was. Obviously you wouldn't like women to think you were past it.' McHale choked with annoyance. He had no wish to be compared with Lill, either in age or in inclinations. 'Anyway, the answer is *yes*. She liked men. She could attract them too—a certain type. No harm in that, so long as Dad was happy.'

'And was he?'

'So far as I know. I don't think he even noticed . . .'

'Was there much to notice?'

'Well, I'm not saying she was Cleopatra or anything. Still, he could have asked questions about all those visits to the Corbys. And I'd have kept my eye on that Guy Fawcett next door. He's been pinching my bottom since they moved here, and making some pretty direct propositions. Still, what the eye doesn't see . . .'

'You're quite sure he suspected nothing?'

Debbie shrugged. She felt no inclination to fight for any member of her family. None of them had fought for her. 'Never gave any sign, that's all I'm saying. Not a great one at registering emotions, my dad.'

McHale decided on the direct approach.

'You seem to have a sort of mark . . . a little bruise, by your left eye.'

Debbie rubbed it unconcernedly. 'Yes?'

'It wasn't the result of some . . . quarrel?'

'Good Lord no. What makes you think that? I was bending down in the bathroom to pick up the toothpaste, and when I straightened up I caught my head on the edge of the bathroom cabinet. It hurt like hell.' She laughed. 'I told them at school I'd been fighting with Mum. It made a good story.'

McHale felt a spasm of frustration pass through him. The cunning little minx! Covering herself in advance in every direction! But he'd pin her down soon enough.

'Ah, I see,' he said easily. 'You were upstairs, weren't you, when the news of your mother's death was brought to your dad. Had you been there all evening?'

'That's right. I was doing my homework. I had a French essay to write.'

'And it took you all the evening? You didn't go down for a snack? Or to watch something on the telly —there was a Francis Durbridge on.'

'The television?' Debbie queried, as though she were rebuking him. 'No. I don't watch much television. That's mostly for old people.'

'Ah! That puts me in my place, doesn't it? So you stayed in your bedroom all evening. And then your

dad came *up,* didn't he, and told you about your
mum. He didn't call you down. That seems a little
odd, doesn't it?'

'Well, naturally, he wouldn't want me to hear in
front of all those coppers, would he? What's odd
about that? Did you think my dad wouldn't have that
much delicacy?'

She had neatly checkmated him. There was no possible follow-up to that put-down. In spite of which,
clenching his teeth, McHale told himself that Debbie
was not a girl of any great intelligence.

McHale had made a home-life for himself that was
hygienic and orderly. His house—'sixties neo-Queen
Anne—on the outskirts of Cumbledon was rather
more pretentious than his income at the time of ac-
quiring it had warranted: it had been bought in the
expectation of that promotion which, in its unduly
laggardly way, had eventually arrived. By now its
garden was stocked with evenly trimmed box hedges,
like plump guardsmen; its paths were as if drawn
with a schoolboy's geometry set; its flowers flourished
and faded in the appropriate seasons—or else.

His wife was an admirable helpmate. She admired
him very much. She entertained the right people when
he suggested it, and served better wine than they were
used to with conventional dishes she knew they liked.
The children were well disciplined, and taught to be
demonstrably affectionate to their father when he
came home. If they said cute things during the day,
Sheila McHale taught them to say them again in the
evening to their father, so that he felt he was the
first to hear them, and could repeat them next day on
duty. As a housewife she fulfilled all the expectations

he had had when, after due consideration, he had asked her to marry him. The house was always spotlessly clean and seemed to run itself, and she had a wonderful repertory of meals suitable for a man who came in at all hours and needed to feel cherished.

When he arrived home that night he went upstairs to kiss the kids goodnight (they woke up specially), and then he settled down to a good casserole which somehow was not overdone. Afterwards he expanded on the sofa, a brandy on the table by his right hand, his wife snuggled temperately up beside him.

'How's this new case?'

'Oh—' he paused for due consideration—'not overexciting, perhaps. But interesting in its way. Ordinary housewife, cheap as dirt; middle-aged, but still something of a looker. Lively—something of a hotpants too.' He smiled apologetically to emphasize that he was using the language of her world, not of theirs. 'The question is: was it someone who knew her, or was it just plain murder in the course of robbery?'

'Did she have much on her?'

'Don't know yet. That's one of the interesting points. In any case, if it was a sort of mugging, it's not likely the murderer would know. She made a bit of a show, in a cheap and nasty kind of way. He may have been taken in by appearances and expected more than he actually got.'

'Not enough for murder, though, you'd have thought?'

'You just can't say these days. They're kinky, these young people: they start in on someone, then they go the whole hog. Not like the old days, when they had the fear of the rope in front of them.'

McHale always talked of 'the fear of the rope' rather than 'hanging'. It had a poetic ring.

'Is that what you think happened?'

'Well, on the whole, yes. And if that's the case, there's not much we can do but wait till he tries it again—apart from chasing up all the possibles on our books and keeping an eye on them.' His good-looking face crinkled in thought, and he took a sip of brandy. 'But it would be fatal to rule out the other possibilities. You've only got to look at the body—' his hands sketched vulgar curves, and his wife smiled sympathetically. 'There's no mistaking the type. Something of a handful: dyed scarlet hair, bags of make-up, slapped on, dirt under the nail varnish.' Sheila McHale shivered dutifully. 'Exactly. I wouldn't employ her as a char. But she'd be attractive to some. And she'd know how to work on them, get what she wanted. I'm on to one of them already—though the poor bloody fish of a husband seems not to have caught on, and it's been going on for years. There may have been others.'

'Sounds a nice type.'

'Mmm. By the look of her she'd be something of a troublemaker, to boot: I'd be very surprised if she wasn't cordially loathed by the neighbours.'

'What about the family? What you'd expect?'

'Pretty much. Hubby works in the parks, eldest son works at the shipyard. Not a good class of murder at all.' He smiled as if he had made a joke. 'And they were all well and truly under her thumb.'

'You don't see them as suspects?' She was very good at knowing the track of his thoughts and following them; she was accessory after the fact to all his wrong-

ful arrests, and there had been one or two. McHale
screwed up his mouth.

'Hardly. Dim as hell, frankly, and spineless into
the bargain. And mostly they've got alibis of a sort—
not watertight ones, but the sort of natural, normal
ones that are better in a way.' He suddenly had a
thought. He should have askel Fred details of the
television programmes he said he had watched between eight-thirty and ten. Before he had a chance
to talk to anyone else. He put the thought from him.

'Well,' said his wife. 'It sounds rather a sordid
little murder.'

'Oh, it is,' said McHale. 'Still, it is my first, apart
from the odd manslaughter where there was no
reasonable doubt. I should be able to get some mileage
out of it. I'm looking forward to getting in with the
neighbourhood. I bet there were some suppressed
hatreds at work there. Lill Hodsden would have put
some backs up that I'm sure of.'

He smiled in anticipation. His wife, looking at
him, thought how handsome he looked. She did not
see that touch of heaviness in the face that had made
Brian Hodsden pronounce McHale a stupid man.
She would never see it.

'Yes,' her husband repeated. 'I think I'll enjoy talking to the neighbours.'

CHAPTER 12

FRIENDS AND NEIGHBOURS

A murder in one's immediate vicinity is a sort of test: a test of the dead person; a test of the family of the corpse; a test of the neighbourhood. Suddenly, dormant characteristics are highlighted, rugs are snatched away to reveal the dust that has been shovelled beneath them over the years.

In Windsor Avenue and the surrounding streets, in the houses of plywood tudor and the bungalows of superbeachhut design, first reactions were to whisper about it over back-garden fences. 'Isn't it terrible?' or 'I couldn't believe my ears when I heard.' The last of these was true enough: no one expects murder in the vicinity, unless they live in the hinterlands of savagery, in Kampala or New York. But 'terrible' was to be interpreted loosely: 'shocking', or 'stunning' —not anything implying grief, or that Lill's end was undeserved.

That was the immediate reaction. It was quite soon superseded by the question of what one said about the family, or—more vitally—how one behaved to them. At first people said: 'It must be awful for *them*,' rather as if it hadn't been awful for Lill. But when they thought about things, weighed up all the circumstances, they rather wondered about the Hodsdens.

It wasn't a *nice* thing to have a murder in the family—
'nice' to be interpreted as respectable, or socially ac-
ceptable. And then—of course Lill must have been
killed by one of these muggers you're always reading
about, and why wasn't something done about them?
. . . On the other hand, if she hadn't . . .

After the first couple of days, people who met
one or other of the Hodsdens in the street tended
to gabble quick condolences, and hurry on.

This tendency was increased when Chief Inspector
McHale and his subordinates came among them, probing, prying, asking about Lill, about the Hodsdens,
and about their own relationships with the afflicted
family. It was exciting, everyone would have been
affronted to be left out, but there again, it wasn't
really respectable. You had to pretend you'd found
it unpleasant. After a while opinion on the point
definitely hardened: they remembered that the
Hodsdens, after all, were foreigners. And one and all
they had always said that they were a funny family . . .

Gordon Hodsden met Ann Watson in Todmarsh
High Street on Saturday morning, before the first
wash of generalized sympathy had totally receded.
Not that Ann Watson was affected by tides of senti-
ment in Windsor Avenue: aloof, remote, she wandered through her daily round never letting herself
become part of any community, neither at home nor
at the school where she taught. But even she was not
quite sure how to behave to Gordon Hodsden. There
is nothing for it on these occasions but to take refuge
in cliché.

'I was awfully sorry to hear—' she said, not feeling

it necessary to specify. 'It must have been a terrible shock to you all.'

'It was,' said Gordon. Hypocrite! he said to himself. Liar! 'Somehow Mum was the last person you'd expect that to happen to.'

'Yes, she was,' said Ann Watson. Hypocrite! she said to herself. Liar!

'Of course I know you had your disagreements with her—'

'Oh—nothing. A silly little thing. Best forgotten.'

'—but what I really meant was not that everyone loved her, because I know they didn't, but that she was so bursting with life and energy. And suddenly, just like that, it's all gone.'

Gordon, in his cautious way, was trying to soften down the picture of himself as a fatuous admirer of his mother's talents and charms. Ann Watson did not help him very much.

'It's particularly bad for you, because you were such a close sort of family,' she said.

Gordon felt he had to take another tentative step towards self-liberation. 'Oh, I don't know about that. Pretty much like most, I suppose. We had our ups and downs. Still, give Mum her due: she didn't interfere much. Let us go our own ways.'

'Oh?' said Ann Watson, with just a trace of upward intonation.

'I mean in our personal lives and that . . . We went our own ways, got our own girl-friends . . .' Ann Watson blinked twice at that, and confirmed Gordon's suspicions of what the row with Lill had been about. Christ, he thought, if I ever make it with her, it'll be against all the odds. 'At any rate,' he said, 'one way or another the neighbourhood's going to miss her.'

'She certainly made an impression,' agreed Ann. Gordon grinned cryptically, to tell her they really shared the same opinion on his late departed mother.

'She didn't give the place tone,' he said, 'but she did give it a bit of life. And Todmarsh could do with all the life it can get.'

'What will you do now?'

'Do?'

'Now she's gone. Will you leave the place?'

With a sudden shock of panic Gordon realized that he had not begun to think in those terms. He had to face it: Lill's death was a beginning, not an end. He felt bewildered, adrift. But he squared his shoulders and made an instant decision.

'No, I don't plan to move on, not yet awhile,' he said. 'My roots are here. I expect for a bit we'll go on as we always have. Only we'll have to get used to Mum not being around. It'll take time.'

'Oh yes,' said Ann. 'It'll take all the time in the world.'

Somehow that was not the way Gordon had hoped the interview would end. He did not want Ann Watson to compare in her mind his loss of a mother with her loss of a husband.

Along Windsor Avenue Miss Gaitskell—she whose arse had been so rudely assaulted in words by Lill Hodsden on her last trip down to the shops of Todmarsh—had a satisfying posthumous revenge by inviting Inspector McHale in to have 'just a *small* glass of sherry' and telling him just about everything she knew about the

Hodsdens. The sherry was South African, but the gossip was the real McCoy.

She fussed over him, massive in shape but birdlike in manner, sometimes putting her head on one side as the insidious suggestions flowed out, sometimes bending forward over their glasses and letting fly with the brutal truth.

'Of course, everyone was always sorry for Old Fred—it's funny, he's always called that, even by his own children I believe—but when it comes down to it, he's a poor fish. I like a man to be a man, I must say. Underneath I think everyone does, don't you agree?' McHale assented confidently. 'And of course, that's what's intriguing everyone.'

'Oh?'

'The *difference*.'

'Difference?'

'In Old Fred. He's a new man since she died. Well, half a man. He's like an extra who's suddenly been given a line to speak. Why? Do you think that underneath he's relieved?'

'I've known it like that before with devoted husbands,' said McHale. 'Though it doesn't usually last.'

'No. Very wisely put. He'll be as dim and lost as ever within six weeks. Or married again to the same type. Still—intriguing. Then there's the Other Man in her life.'

'Ah yes—'

'You know already, I see. How, I wonder? The family told you, perhaps? Who? The boys? Gordon knew it couldn't be kept under cover, I suppose. Well, Corby's been looking like death warmed up since Thursday. He's talking of closing the yard and retiring to a cottage. A cottage not too far from a pub, I imagine. You've talked to him already, I expect?'

'Just on the 'phone—about when she left the house that night. I'll be going back to him, inevitably, when I've pinned down exactly what sort of relationship there was between him and Mrs Hodsden.'

'You could ask him about the colour TV the Hodsdens have—and probably lots of other things she'd screwed out of him that we haven't heard about. She told someone she was thinking of getting a car, and you can be sure it wasn't Hodsden money was going to buy it. There is no Hodsden money, I know that for a fact. They blew what little they had buying that lump of a son out of the army.'

'Were there any other boy-friends, would you say?'

'Hmmm. Probably. But I've no evidence. If a guess is any use to you I'd say try Achituko and that Guy Fawcett.'

'Akki—?'

'Achituko. From the Coponawi Islands—Pacific, you know.' Her big body softened, as if she became sentimental at the thought of Todmarsh's token black. 'He's a nice boy; exceptionally polite. Still, you wouldn't expect good taste from someone like that, not our taste, would you? And I'm sure there's *some*-thing with him and the Hodsdens. Fawcett's only moved into the road in the last year. The sort of man who makes respectable women itch to have a good wash. Put that type next door to a Lill Hodsden and the result is as predictable as strikes next winter.'

'I'll certainly keep them in mind,' said McHale, fixing her with his gaze of professional appreciation. 'Is there anyone who had cause to hate Lill Hodsden, would you say, around here?'

'Well, we none of us liked her. None of us had cause to.' Miss Gaitskell blushed slightly as the insult to her posterior came back to her mind. 'When she was in a good mood she was tolerable for five minutes. When she wasn't—we scattered! I know for sure she had a row with Mrs Carstairs.'

'Oh yes?'

'Because she was muttering to me about it next day. We were comparing notes. She'd had Lill Hodsden up to the ears. But she wouldn't make it clear what the row was about.'

'Anyone else who hated her?'

Miss Gaitskell's eyes sharpened, as she hazarded a guess that had nagged at her mind all day: 'You could try the family,' she said.

But McHale did not bite. 'I've seen the family,' he said. 'At the moment I'm more interested in the neighbours.'

So Miss Gaitskell filled his glass, and resuming her bird-like stance told him more and more about the neighbours, though she would dearly have liked to wonder aloud about the Hodsdens. But at the end McHale was well satisfied with his morning's work. He could not have picked his informant better. Obviously an ex-postmistress had ways peculiar to herself of finding things out.

Guy Fawcett, home at midday and looking for all his burly frame oddly gaunt, turned out of his front gate and walked along Windsor Avenue to the brown painted house two doors down. Uncertainly, for him, he trailed down the stone-dashed side path and knocked tentatively on the back door. He wasn't look-

ing forward to this. Mrs Casey, square, black and off-
putting, opened the door and eyed him sourly.

'Yes?'

'Oh, er, Mrs Casey, we haven't actually met, but
I'm Guy Fawcett from number eight.'

'I know,' muttered Mrs Casey sepulchrally, as if
the lack of formal introduction had not stopped her
marking him down for damnation in her little black
book.

'I wondered if we could just have a little talk
about a certain matter . . .'

'Yes?'

'Could we go inside, do you think?'

'I've nothing to say that can't be said on my own
doorstep.'

'Yes, well, I have. Please . . .' She gazed at him with
the flame of hell lividly present behind the arctic grey
of her eyes. Then she stood silently aside. Guy scut-
tled past her into the kitchen, and wedged himself
gracelessly into a kitchen chair. Mrs Casey stood by
her back door and waited.

'It's this business of what went on . . . what you
saw the other day . . . Tuesday . . . in the garden,'
said Guy Fawcett, stumbling over his words and becoming even sweatier and nastier than usual. He
hadn't behaved or felt like this since his headmaster had been more than usually insistent on hearing
precisely what he had been doing with little Sally
Foster in the boys' lavatories after schooltime. Mrs
Casey, like his headmaster, had an impressive line in
silence, and gave him not an inch of leeway.

'Of course it didn't mean anything . . . what you
saw. Just a bit of silly fun. Meant nothing at all. But
I'd be glad if you didn't mention it to the police.'

'Oh?'

'You see, people misinterpret that sort of thing.' Something like a malevolent laugh escaped Mrs Casey. 'And I'm a married man—a good husband too, very fond of my wife. You understand, I wouldn't want her to get hurt. And she'd take it very hard if it got round to her that . . . that . . .'

Mrs Casey sniffed, which seemed to mean that she very much doubted whether Mrs Fawcett would care a jot.

'And then there's your daughter—that was. I don't suppose you'd want to blacken the reputation of your own daughter—'

'She blackened her own.'

'Well, even if that were true, which I don't own, you'd have to be a funny mother to want to blacken it further.'

'I can't compromise with the truth.'

Guy's voice rose. 'I'm not asking you to compromise with the truth. I'm asking you to keep your trap shut when the police question you.' He was getting both irritated and querulous, as he always did when things went against him. It was one of his least attractive moods. 'We all know this thing was done by a mugger. But that won't stop them raking around in your daughter's private life if they feel like it. And if they do that they might find more dirty linen than even *you* would like to see hung out in public.'

'Oh? You think so?'

'I know so. You take it from me.' He slowed up, and began to alter his tone. 'And you'd better remember that if you say anything about me and her to the cops, I'll be the first to spill the beans.' Mrs Casey seemed for the first time to falter in her ada-

mantine stance by the door, like a guardsman about
to crumble at the knees. Guy sensed his advantage
and weighed in. 'Like the details about Debbie and
that Achituko, for a start. There's more dirt in that
family than just Lill's dirt.'

Mrs Casey flinched, and looked as if she would demand what he meant. But that would have been stoop-
ing to his level, and Mrs Casey never stooped. Her
mouth was working, with an expression of distaste:
she seemed to find his presence in her kitchen repel-
lent, demeaning. Miss Gaitskell was right about Fawcett's effect upon respectable women. Mrs Casey
closed her eyes, thought hard and long, and then
said:

'If they asked me a question, I'd have to tell them.
Being police. It wouldn't be right otherwise. But if
they don't ask, I'll let the matter be.'

Guy Fawcett breathed out, summoned up a greasy
smile, and made straight for the door. 'That's all I
wanted,' he said. Unable to leave without reasserting
his masculine advantage he added with an attempt at
satire: 'Just so long as you don't regard it as com-
promising with the truth, of course.'

Passing briefly in Snoggers Alley in the early after-
noon sun, Debbie and Achituko paused, just momentarily, as if for condolences.

'Wednesday?' muttered Debbie.

'If Mrs Carstairs goes out,' muttered Achituko. 'I
think she suspects. Will they let you?'

'Who's to stop me now?' said Debbie with a smile
of new-minted triumph, and went on her way.

* * *

'I hear my *friend* Mrs Hodsden has been murdered.'

His wife's words from the bed caused Wilf Hamilton Corby to give a start worthy of a sneak villain in a silent film, and almost to drop his wife's lunch tray, which he was carrying downstairs.

He had, after all, made sure that Friday's *South Wessex Chronicle* held no word of Thursday night's event. His wife never listened to the radio, so she could have heard it on no local bulletin. The cleaning lady had not been in since Thursday morning. He himself had said, and intended to say, nothing.

But Drusilla Corby spoke the literal truth. Todmarsh—boring, moribund Todmarsh—was speaking of nothing else. And lying on her bed, reading her never ending supply of books from Cumbledon Public Library ('I can read *anything*,' she would declare, 'except love stories,' and she would look viciously at her husband as she said it) she had had the gossip of two shrill-voiced neighbours wafted in by the breeze through the open window.

'You never told me,' she pursued, dangerously feline, 'about the death of my good friend.'

'Didn't want to upset you,' muttered Wilf, looking as if he wanted to make a dash for it.

'Why should it upset me, though, I wonder?' she asked, her mouth twisted and ugly as she looked towards the ceiling for inspiration. 'I've never to my knowledge set eyes on the woman.'

Wilf Corby cleared his throat. 'Murder's always upsetting,' he hazarded. 'Didn't want you to hear—'

'But you know I *dote* on murder! Murder's my greatest stimulant!' She flapped a pudgy paw at the pile of books on her dressing-table. 'In fiction, as second best to fact.'

'You wouldn't like murder as close as this.'

'Close?'

'Just down the road here. Hardly any distance—'

'Really? Now isn't that odd? My best friend killed within a few hundred yards of my own house.' A spasm of genuine irritation crossed her perpetually discontented face. 'Thursday night. How annoying. I took one of my draughts. Otherwise I would have heard all the fun . . . Did you hear all the fun, Wilf?'

'I watched telly. Then I turned in early.'

'Not much of an alibi. Still, you hardly need one . . . or do you? And how was she killed?'

'Strangled, they say.'

'They say strangled, do they?' The voice caressed the word oddly. 'Would any great strength be required, do they say?'

'Average. Moderate.'

'You're hardly in condition, are you, these days, Wilf? Not even average. Not even moderate. But your hands are carpenter's hands—I remember them so well.' She shivered ostentatiously. 'Rough. Calloused. That was before they started to shake.'

'Is there anything you want?'

'Want? Oh no. I shall enjoy myself now. Just lying here and thinking. In the course of time, perhaps, I shall want to talk to the police.'

'Police be buggered,' Corby shouted. 'You'll do no such thing.'

'Coarse as always. And still imagining you rule the roost. Really, Wilf, you never do have the last word— you should know that by now.'

The voice died away to show she was content to leave it at that. Wilf Hamilton Corby fussed off downstairs, fuming impotently. Drusilla Corby lay back, her pink filmy nightdress emphasizing the bony fragility of her body, the odd pudgy hands clutching the turned-over top of her sheets. She gazed at the ceiling, the day-long screen of her own thoughts and plans, with a smile on her wide, unlikeable mouth and a sparkle in her black-rimmed eyes.

CHAPTER 13

FRED AND FAMILY

'Everyone's been very good,' said Fred, looking meditatively at the knife which had just carved its way through an underboiled potato.

'What makes you say that?' said Gordon aggressively. Everything Fred said these days became the subject for scrutiny or contradiction. As though they were competing in some way—over a woman, or a patch of land.

'All the sympathy. Everyone's had a word to say.'

'And hurried on double quick when they've said it.'

'That's natural,' said Brian, desperately fed up with this petty bickering and anxious to avoid another futile uprush of temper. 'People do find death—well, sort of embarrassing.'

'More especially murder,' said Debbie flatly.

It was the first time the word had been used in the family. Killed, after all, is an expression that clutches a few shreds of ambiguity around its bareness. Murder says it all. Trust Debbie to be the one to use it.

Sunday dinner, even before that, had not been going well. Debbie, who took after her mother in so little, walked doggedly in her footsteps as a cook. But they had had to accept gratefully from Lill; Debbie aroused no such intincts of cowardly acquiescence.

In fact they all felt vaguely hostile towards her, even before the blushing pink pork chops and the cricket-ball potatoes: it was almost as if they thought her delinquencies had led to Lill's death, though consciously they knew this was not so. And anyway two of them, at least, had no objection to Lill's death.

'The fact is,' said Gordon, 'we're an embarrassment to people. They don't know how to behave. I expect it'll be like that for months. Or until the police nail someone.'

'Shouldn't be long now,' said Fred, chewing, as well he might, a nasty piece of underdone pork. 'That Mc-Hale isn't one to let the grass grow under his feet, I'll be bound. Looked a capable chappie.'

'He could probably spot a parking offence at twenty feet,' said Brian.

Fred blinked. 'No call to be sarky. You young people are so sharp these days you cut yourselves. Remember it's your mother's death he's investigating. And I say he'll get him.'

'Well, let's hope he gets him double quick,' said Gordon. 'I don't like the way people are looking at us.'

'I was wondering,' said Fred, the old uncertainty taking over from the new, almost confident self, 'if I might just slip out and have a drink tonight. Of course, it wouldn't have done last night, not a Saturday, but Sundays is always a quiet night . . . it's very *quiet* always, of a Sunday . . . I don't know. What do you think?'

'Providing you choose a very *quiet* pub,' said Brian satirically.

'Oh, I would,' said Fred, missing the satire in his haste to clutch the straw. 'I know it sounds downright heartless, but I missed my pint last night.'

'Anybody'd think we were in the nineteenth century,' complained Debbie. 'Life doesn't stop, just because . . . she's gone. I'm going out tonight, anyway.'

'Where?' Gordon's voice rapped out, sharp and loud.

'Mind your own business, nosey.'

'None of your lip,' cut in Fred. 'I'm your father and I've a right to know.'

'Well, he's my brother, and he can mind his own business. If you want to know I'm going round to Karen Dawson's like I always do on Sundays. Any more questions?'

'Just you mind your tongue, my girl,' said Fred, getting up and beginning to stump off to the living-room to doze in front of the television. 'Now your mum's gone it's me 'as got to keep an eye on you. It's plain as the nose on your face that you need it.'

As he closed the kitchen door, Debbie put her finger to her nose in a gesture of derision.

'Look, my girl,' said Gordon, turning the whole force of his personality on her and fixing her with an angry, smouldering stare, 'let's get this straight. There's nothing changed by Mum's death as far as you're concerned. You've been disgracing us, and you're going to take the consequences now. You've got to account for all your movements, and be in by ten o'clock every night. We want to know where you are and who you're with. And if you so much as exchange a word with that black bastard, you'll be locked up in your room like you were on Thursday.'

'Gordon—' warned Brian.

'Oh, don't worry, Bri. I'm not bothered by Gordon,' said Debbie, unconcernedly inspecting her nails.

'I know him too well: he's muscle-covered cotton-wool. He's all bluster and no guts.'

'You little bitch!' Gordon grabbd her by the wrists and twisted her hands down on to the table. 'Look at me, damn you! Someone's got to get you in hand, and if it's not old Fred then it's going to be me—'

'You can shout and bully as much as you like,' said Debbie, returning his gaze with equal intensity. 'But I know you. Did any of you protect me from Mum when she was alive? You all saw her picking on me, and you did bugger all. I respect Brian more than you because he doesn't pretend to be anything else but a mother's boy. You're both milksops at heart. Why should I take any notice of a gutless pair like you? The only person who rules my life now is me.'

She got up from the table and took herself over to the door. ' 'Bye, Brian. Enjoy the washing-up.'

'Little bitch,' said Gordon under his breath. 'I'll show her who's boss. She's been running wild. If we don't rein her in she'll be the talk of the town.'

'Well, Mum's methods never did much good,' said Brian.

'Who's going to use Mum's methods? I'll come down on her a damn sight harder than Mum ever did if I catch her with that Achituko.'

Brian, pensively clearing away, said nothing for a bit. Obviously Gordon in this sort of a mood was past reasoning with. But when he did speak, what he said was not to Gordon's liking: 'In the long run I don't suppose we can do much about it. She'll soon be seventeen. And it's probably not all that important.'

'Not important! A girl of that age sleeping with a bloody black!'

'What age did you have your first girl, Gordon?'

'You know bloody well that's different.'

'What bothers you is that he's black.'

'Too right it bothers me, and it would you too if you hadn't got all those namby-pamby notions you educated buggers get. But that's not the only thing. If she goes on the way she's going now, she'll be the town bike before she's twenty. She'll be dropping 'em so fast there'll be scorch marks on her thighs. She'll make us the laughing-stock of the town. What this family needs is a bit of discipline.'

Brian thought sadly to himself: I don't think that's what I need. He said: 'What do you think the police are doing? Have you heard any rumours?'

'Talking to the neighbours as far as I know.'

'Do you think they'll get anywhere?'

Gordon shrugged, still hunched over the table and puffing at a cigarillo. 'Maybe. I'd have thought it was pretty sure to be one of them, if it's not a mugger. Or Corby. Or—God knows, there were enough who hated her.'

'If it wasn't one of the family,' said Brian quietly, scrubbing at a plate with his mop.

'Oh, for Christ's sake!' said Gordon, stubbing out his fag. 'We've been over this already. Who've you got in mind now? Fred again? He hasn't got the strength.'

'You think strength's just a matter of being big, and being in training. It's not. Fred may be small, but he's been a gardener for thirty years and more.'

'Look, Bri,' said Gordon, getting up and coming at Brian from behind, turning him round to get his words across, 'you know and I know that Fred never made a decision in the whole of his married life. He's bloody feebleminded. Then all of a sudden he makes a decision to murder Lill. Don't be bloody potty.'

'Debbie could have done it.'

'Debbie was locked in.'

'Debbie had a duplicate key in the room. She's practically admitted it. She could have sneaked out any time if Fred was dozing. Come to that, Grandma Casey could have done it.'

Gordon let out a great hoot of laughter. 'Oh my Lord! That really takes the cake, that does! Poor old Gran at seventy-five strangling her own daughter!'

'She's as strong as an ox.'

'She wields a hefty rolling-pin, that's about the extent of her strength. You don't seem to realize, baby brother, that strangling someone isn't like tying a knot in a bit of string. And what the hell *is* this, anyway? Why this sudden urge to prove one of us is a murderer?'

Brian swallowed and turned back to the sink. 'We were going to do it,' he said. 'Or we said we were going to do it.'

'We *were* going to.'

'Perhaps it runs in the family.'

'Oh my God,' muttered Gordon. 'This is like some . . . some ruddy superstition. "Keep away from that family—there's bad blood there." Give over. That's just melodramatic.'

'Well,' said Brian, 'I tell you I won't be happy until they've got him. As it is, I just look around, at us, and I think—'

'You think too bleeding much. It's none of us. I can think of three or four who're more likely than us.'

'Who then?'

'That black. Old Corby. Fawcett next door.'

'I hope you're right, that's all.'

'Of course I'm right. Meanwhile we've got to present a front . . . as a family. Keep up our public image. Give them the idea we're one big happy family, temporarily desolated by the loss of our beloved mum. And I tell you I'm not having Debbie destroying that by playing hotpants with a wog. I'm not having *anybody* stepping out of line—get me?'

He walked to the door, then turned and insistently repeated: 'See?' Brian nodded miserably, seeing Gordon's point but hating his way of putting it. Then, desolately, he trailed through after him towards the sitting-room, through the door of which they could hear the television going.

'Forget it,' hissed Gordon. 'You're just getting the willies. Come on—there's athletics on the telly.'

He opened the door. The set was going full blast, and in the armchair Fred was snoozing, mouth open, with the Sunday paper over his face.

'Look!' said Gordon. 'The head of the family.'

By the time McHale came to interview Mrs Casey she was so upset by her apprehensions of scandal in the Hodsden family and uncertainties about the morally correct course to take that he found something very different from her usual rocklike self. In fact, she was butter in his hands.

Of course he had the advantage of knowing the type. Every policeman knew the type. After a mugging, or a bank raid, the only totally reliable source of information would generally be a Mrs Casey—

someone whose sharp eye was undimmed, whose brain was unfuddled by excess, who took in better than any camera the colour of the attacker's shoes, whether he wore a moustache or glasses, his approximate height. The Mrs Caseys of this world see, register, collate and disapprove.

So, after trailing through the details of her activities on Thursday night—all irreproachable and quite uncheckable—McHale leaned forward in his armchair, in the specially opened front room, redolent of pre-war Leicester and enshrining relics of Alfred Casey, plumber, departed, and said in a solemn voice:

'I think you and I have something in common, ma'am. I think we both have standards!'

He really believed it. He would never have understood that, though their opinions might sometimes overlap, his standards were a mere assemblage of conventionalities that happened to boost his self-love and his vision of his own place in the universal scheme of things; whereas in her there remained, however perverted by the straitjacket of nonconformity, some sense of a Deity who had to be served, irrespective of personal inclination.

Mrs Casey nodded grimly and said: 'Aye. There's not so many has standards these days.'

'That was what I was meaning,' said McHale. He paused.

'I don't know where I went wrong,' said Mrs Casey, ruminating as she caught his line of thought. 'But go wrong I did.'

'You shouldn't blame yourself,' said McHale.

'Who else is there to blame? Alf—that was my husband—was hardly ever home, not during t'war and after. And you can't blame the father for how a daughter turns out.'

'You must have seen a lot of things, things that went on next door, that pained you?'

Mrs Casey nodded—but with a hint of wariness.

'I should tell you that we have a pretty good idea that your daughter had—shall we say boy-friends? The name of Wilf Hamilton Corby has come up.'

She seemed to breathe out. 'There's plenty could have told you that. That's no great discovery.'

'Precisely. But then there are the other names. This Mr Achituko, for example.'

'Not *her*,' said Mrs Casey, then pulled herself up. 'I've no evidence Lill ever went outside her own colour.'

McHale registered the moment, but imperceptibly. 'And then some people have mentioned the next-door neighbour, Mr Fawcett.'

Mrs Casey looked straight ahead of her.

'What would you say to that?'

'You haven't asked me anything.'

'Do you think your daughter was—carrying on with Mr Fawcett?'

Mrs Casey choked. 'I can't tell a lie,' she muttered. And really she almost couldn't. 'I—I think she was.'

'What makes you think so? Did you see anything?'

And suddenly a great tear welled up at the sides of Mrs Casey's eyes, and she gulped back a sob. 'I don't know what's for the best,' she cried. 'He's *wicked*. Coming to me like that.'

'Don't you think,' said McHale, leaning forward with a gentleness whose genuineness she was not in a position to examine, 'that it's always best to tell the whole truth?'

The tawdry truism went straight to Mrs Casey's methodistical heart, with its impulse for open public confession. Since Guy Fawcett's visit she had been unhappy about covering the family shame with lies and concealments. She was not even sure what she was concealing. McHale's simplistic appeal went straight to her heart.

'She was a dreadful woman, my daughter!' she wailed. 'A scandal and a shame! To think that any woman could *throw* herself like that at a man—practically *asking* to be . . . to be made wicked! And a man like him, too! And Fred thinking her the perfect wife!'

And then it all came out. The scene in the garden, the retreat to the house, and what she imagined went on in the house. And then Guy Fawcett's visit to her, and his threats. And then, under McHale's gentle probing, the implications about Debbie and Mr Achituko.

'But there can't be anything there, can there?' she cried. 'Debbie's just a little girl. It must be something in his horrible mind!'

'I'm sure it is,' said McHale soothingly. 'Just don't worry your head about it. You feel better now you've had a good cry, don't you?'

And certainly she did. He could see she did. When he went to his car he felt much like a parish priest who has just shriven a particularly tough sinner in his flock. And his mind was buzzing with the names of Corby and Fawcett, of Achituko and Debbie Hodsden.

* * *

Brian, at the sitting-room window, watched McHale
leaving his gran's, and felt a dull sense of being inside
a net, a net contracting with every day that passed.

The family was in danger of breaking up. He could
see it coming, all the time. Not on the surface. Everything was normal on the surface. Debbie was out at
her friend's—going off half an hour since, turning
ostentatiously in the opposite direction from Achituko's lodging and walking down the road with indecent
perkiness. Gordon had put on his track suit and gone
on a training run. Fred had more or less woken up—
how much sleep he seemed to need these days!—and
was attempting the *Sunday Grub* crossword. He had
filled in the answers to three clues, probably wrongly.

But underneath everything was cracking up. Debbie and Gordon were at war, just as Debbie and Lill
had always been. Fred was making foredoomed attempts to assert himself, and would soon retire, defeated and resentful, before Gordon's greater force
of personality. He, Brian—he, Brian . . .

He, Brian, was wondering if things hadn't been
better on the whole with Lill alive. He was scanning
the past to see whether there hadn't been happy
times then as well. Lill and her boys at the Fair, twice
a year regular, when the fair came to Todmarsh. Lill
and her boys at Torquay, walking up the beach and
scandalizing the residents.

Had it been so bad? Hadn't it been *something,*
some stable centre, which was now missing, leaving
him lost and bewildered? Was it so dreadful, Lill's
ghastly vulgarity, which raked the beaches of Tunisia
with its screeching laughter and drew forth the
shivering distaste of the other British holidaymakers?

Brian remembered Tunisia, and stirred uneasily in his chair. Remembered the sun, the camel rides, the endless sands. Remembered the tightness in his chest, like an intimation of mortality. Remembered Fred wandering lost around the grounds of the hotel, grateful for a casual word thrown in his direction. Remembered Gordon making up to a gross German Frau, bathing topless under stony Moslem gazes. Remembered the lemons and the figs, the little Arab cakes, the Berber women in town . . .

Remembered the boys who danced around them as they walked past the medina—their handstands, their importunities, their mocking imitations, and their haunting, inviting cries: '*Voulez-vous coucher avec ma sœur?*'

And then: *Êtes-vous anglais? Voulez-vous coucher avec mon frère?*'

CHAPTER 14

THE TWA CORBIES

Wilf Hamliton Corby did all he knew how to stop his wife getting in touch with the police. The cleaning lady came on Mondays, and, purchasing her loyalty with a five-pound note. Wilf impressed upon her that on no account was she to ring them if his wife asked her to. He also told her to stick around the house till he got home. 'Sick fancies,' he said: 'that's what she's got—sick fancies.'

But he was no match for his wife. Drusilla Corby sent the char down to the shop with another five-pound note for a box of tissues: 'Keep the change— you've been so good to me,' she said, with a smile that would have made the Albert Memorial blanch. The char found she might have multiple loyalties, and trotted off obediently. Then Drusilla Corby simply rose from her bed and tottered interestingly downstairs to the telephone. Wilf Hamilton Corby, had he seen, might have regarded it as a miracle of nearly New Testament proportions, but then he knew almost as little about his wife's condition as we know about the gentleman who took up his bed in that interesting volume. Within ten minutes of the phone call Chief Inspector McHale was ensconced in an uncomfortable reproduction Chippendale chair, prepared for the goods.

Mrs Corby regarded him speculatively from her bed. Not as a man, or as any kind of sexual object. She had never greatly liked men, and her marriage had by now contributed to a positive aversion. She regarded McHale solely from the point of view of the degree of discomfort, fear and sheer panic he might induce in her husband. And she thought that— properly worked on—he would do very well. She saw an element of the bully, the respectable moral thug in McHale, and she liked what she saw.

'I suppose you're wondering what made me call you,' she said, her voice soft with physical weakness.

'People do still call us, even in this day and age, when they have information,' said McHale.

'I mean what I suppose you'd call my *motive*,' said Drusilla Corby. 'I'm sure there *are* still public-spirited people in the world, but I'm quite sure I couldn't claim to be one of them. I'm not even a good wife, or perhaps I would have held back. I'm afraid all my motives would seem to you intolerably vengeful. I have to tell you, Inspector, that the reason I am—like this—is that my husband . . . But I won't go into details. Much better not. I merely give you the hint so that you won't think me mentally sick, as well as physically—destroyed!'

'There's no question of that, Mrs Corby,' said McHale, whose sympathy was marginally more genuine than her story. 'I can see that you've suffered.'

'So much! But that's enough of that subject. I wanted to see you, and talk to you, because I knew you would have heard by now about my connection with this—this creature that has been murdered.'

'I had heard,' said McHale cautiously, 'that Mrs Hodsden was a friend of yours.'

'False!' said Mrs Corby, with whiplash scorn. 'I never set eyes on the woman in my life.' She paused. 'And do you have the impression, Inspector, that Lill Hodsden was the *kind* of woman likely to be *my* friend?'

'The point had struck me as odd,' admitted McHale.

'Ah, you have realized, have you, that she was a creature of quite stupendous vulgarity? Very perceptive of you. And whatever else may be said of me, I am not that. I am comforted that you understand—but now I have seen you I realize you were bound to. I think Mrs Hodsden's connection with this house will be quite plain to you when you meet my husband. Like clings to like, they say, don't they? And those two certainly did cling.'

'What you are saying, then, ma'am, is that Mrs Hodsden came to this house solely to see your husband, never to visit you.'

'Precisely. She came to minister to his sexual needs —needs of a minimal and totally ridiculous nature, I would conjecture. She came on Monday and Thursday nights, regular as clockwork, and—doubly insulting—she had her own key, and went straight through to the study, where these acts of passion took place.'

Mrs Corby leaned back against her pillow and cultivated her fragile invalid look. In fact she was bewildered by her impulse to swing between two roles, that of bitch (which came naturally) and that of pathetic victim of a brutal man's aggression (which was a rarer assumption). Like most people shut away from society at large, she was not in the habit of pre-

paring faces to meet the people that she met. But Mc-
Hale barely noticed her amateur dramatic assump-
tions. He was too interested in what she was saying.

'So in fact,' he said, 'these visits on Mondays and
Thursdays were exclusively to your husband, were
they?'

'Certainly. How monotonously regular they were,
weren't they? Even Shakespeare couldn't have made
much out of two hours on Mondays and Thursdays.'

'Do you know anything more about the visits?'

'Certainly. First of all, she exacted her price. Gifts
at first. Money now and then, on an irregular basis.
She was also starting to mention marriage.'

'What!'

'Precisely. Bizarre in the circumstances, isn't it? But
that is exactly what she did on Monday night.'

'And did your husband seem of the same mind?'

'I have nothing but contempt for Wilf Corby,' enun-
ciated his wife, gazing ahead like a dyspeptic Jane
Austen as she made the judgment; 'In general he has
the brains of a lemming. But even I will admit that
were he to divorce me or encompass my death (which
he will not, because he hasn't got the nerve) he would
not be foolish enough to do it in order to marry Lill
Hodsden.'

'Still,' said McHale, 'that's a bit of a stunner.'

'Quite. And that,' said Drusilla Corby, 'is why he
tried to buy her off, I wouldn't mind betting.'

'Buy her off?'

'My other piece of information. My last, I'm
afraid. Shut away up here one is so . . . out of
things. But this I do know. It was on Thursday
night . . .'

'The night of the murder?'

'As I now know. She arrived, I suspect, in a temper. She slammed the door of the study, a thing she'd never done before. Wilf was up here with me, fussing around the bedroom as usual. When the door slammed he muttered "wind"—just the sort of idiotic lie he would jump into, since it was a perfectly still night. Anyway, he went down, and I heard nothing for a bit. But half an hour before she was due to go—she *always* went at half past nine—I heard the study door open and Wilf walk through to the lounge. The lounge is little used these days, as you can imagine, and I wondered what he could be doing. There's a fine old cabinet there, wonderful craftsmanship and solid as rock. It holds a lot of china and glass—stuff I inherited, wasted on *him*. In the bottom section my jewels are kept. I have no use for them now, a worn-out old invalid woman—no, no, don't protest. Anyway, I *know* he opened the cabinet: I can't mistake that sound. I *think* I heard him get out my jewel case and rummage in my jewellery. And that seems the most likely reason he'd go to the cabinet: that painted creature would have had no use for fine china.'

'I see.'

'Now do you understand why I called you? Rifling *my* jewel-box for something to placate his ill-tempered whore?'

'I can understand very well. But there is one thing: there was no jewellery of any consequence on the body.'

'Was there not? Certainly if there was cheap stuff he didn't get it from *my* jewel-box. I'd like to think he fobbed her off with something cheap, because it would be so easy to do, but that doesn't seem to fit the facts . . .' She meditated eagerly and came up with the most damaging of all possible explanations. 'Do you think he could have killed her to get it back?'

'Hmm,' said McHale, who wasn't happy with a murder for that sort of motive a bare ten minutes after the jewel had been given. 'I wouldn't want to commit myself. You've certainly provided me with food for thought—and a possible motive for *someone*.'

'I'm glad you think so. You know my husband has been sweating *blood* these last few days.'

'Really? Well, he won't have to do that much longer. You're sure there's nothing else you have to tell me?'

Mrs Corby squirmed restlessly in her bed, greedy for the attention and excitement McHale provided her with. 'I wish there was. But there's nothing. I'm so cut off up here. Day after day, nothing but silence.' She sighed, an April breeze through a willow tree.

'I should have thought it was remarkable how much you managed to . . . be aware of,' said McHale.

'Sometimes,' said Drusilla Corby, switching roles, 'I manage to *totter* to the top of the stairs.'

A quick trip to the Station put McHale in touch with the forensic people in Cumbledon. He had thought it all out in the car: it was possible Corby had loaded Lill with necklaces or rings but on the whole McHale doubted it. Necklaces were difficult to explain away, and rings were nastily ambiguous. Natural parsimony would tempt him to get away with less if he could, and on the whole a brooch seemed more the ticket.

It proved a lucky hit. The lab people confirmed that on Lill's pre-Raphaelite green dress, under her

leopard-skin coat, were two minute holes that probably were the marks of a brooch pin. It might be
worth checking the position of the holes against
Lill's existing jewellery.

But all things considered, McHale thought he could
go for bust without checking. He chuckled with joy
and self-love, sure he was on to something. The constable driving him to the Corby shipyard could feel
the self-approbation oozing out of him, and gazed
darkly ahead: McHale had not made himself loved
in the Todmarsh Station. There was something else
too: the anticipation of pleasure, the Achilles heel
of a policeman about to grill a suspect. McHale's lips
twitched as they pulled up at the yard, for he could
see, watching them from the office, the terrified eyes
of Wilf Corby. But as he got out of the car the first
person who came into his line of vision was Gordon
Hodsden. And Gordon—overalled, dirty from sawdust
and oil—was obviously wanting to waylay him.

'Do you think I could have a word, sir?' he asked.
The 'sir' was deliberate and premeditated. McHale
responded: he looked towards the office, and smiled
at the thought of Wilf Corby waiting inside.

'Certainly,' he said. He glanced in the direction of
a deserted wharf, and together they strolled away
from the massive shed where the boats were built. Mc-
Hale remained courteous but remote, and Gordon
placatory rather than worried.

'I've got to come clean,' he began. 'I wasn't altogether open with you on Friday.'

'No,' said McHale. 'I know you weren't.'

'It's not easy when it's your own sister.'

'It's foolish, whoever it concerns.'

'Anyway, I want to give it to you straight now—'

McHale was not going to let anyone claim virtue on such flimsy grounds. 'You want to give it to me straight now because you know your grandmother has already told me all she knows.'

'Fair enough,' said Gordon, looking him straight in the eye. 'But that's not the whole truth. I couldn't get out of Gran exactly what she said. She was too upset.' He stopped at the end of the wharf and looked sombrely out to sea. 'No, it's not just that; it's something else . . . I suppose you know the basic facts.'

'I've guessed. But you tell me.'

'Mum and Debbie had a row. Debbie got a bit bashed about (not serious—you saw the bruise). She disobeyed Mum, though, and went off to school the next day. Mum was furious with her when she got home, and locked her in her room. We didn't tell you that because we . . . we felt it would give a wrong impression about Mum.'

McHale kept silence. He had a half-sense that Gordon's explanation of their motives for concealment was inadequate.

'The point is this: the row was about Achituko. The bloody black who lives along the road. She'd been sleeping with him.'

McHale sighed. That was better. That was coming cleaner. 'That was what I suspected.'

Gordon whirled round to face him and spoke with a low, controlled intensity: 'The point is, can't you do something about it?'

'Do?'

'Get him out of here. Deported or something. Away from her. Have you talked to him yet?'

'Not yet—all in good time.'

'You should. He and Mum had a row in the street,

couple of hours before she died. He could easily have done her in for revenge. But what I really want is to get the bugger deported. You could manage that. How long have they been sleeping together? We just don't know. She could easily have been under the age of consent when they started. You could get him on that.'

The idea appealed to McHale. In matters of race he had all the innate liberalism of his middle-middle-class, tax-inspecting background. He hated the bastards, and behaved to them with impeccable courtesy. Cutting short Achituko's so-called study at this local so-called university was a notion of delicious appeal to him.

'Bit early to speak of deportation,' he said cautiously. 'Though it's something we could keep in mind. In fact, we could take him in for questioning and on this angle we could definitely give him the works. But I'm not sure what your interest in this is.'

'What do you think? We're going through a difficult time, but we're a decent-enough family.' Gordon turned his dark eyes broodingly out to sea again. 'Now Lill's gone most of the responsibility comes back on me. You've seen Fred. I've got to find some way to keep that little—Debbie in order. She's not going round disgracing us by sleeping with blacks, or anyone else at her age. Christ, you must understand: don't you have a sister?'

'No—but I understand,' said McHale. Gordon Hodsden was articulating attitudes which lay very close to his conformist heart. You didn't hear them so much from the younger generation. In fact, he was beginning to feel a much greater respect for Gordon Hodsden, though he failed to realize this was because Gordon had changed his performance since the earlier interview. 'I'll do what I can.'

'Thanks. I'm very grateful,' said Gordon. And together they trudged up the wharf, watched by supplicating, terrified eyes from the windows of the shipyard offices. As they turned into the yard the eyes disappeared.

When it became clear that McHale was not going away in his nice big car but was coming into the yard proper, Corby oozed out of his office to usher the Inspector in. He was a pathetic sight, but he tickled some little instinct in McHale which made him overlook the pathos: he never disliked the thought of an inquisition, but now he looked forward to this one with positive relish. It was the bonhomous cheeriness of Corby, trying to cover over the beginnings of a piglike sweatiness, that aroused the relish. McHale rationalized it by characterizing Corby in his mind as a savage husband and an adulterer, but he hardly believed the first, and didn't greatly care about the second. It was Corby's craven fear that tickled his inborn relish. He decided to play with him for a bit, catlike.

'I'm sure you understand why it is I'm here,' he said, sitting down opposite the boss's desk.

'Oh yes—perfectly.' Corby puffed and glistened as he sat uneasily in his position of authority. 'You have to follow everything up. I realized you'd want a bit more than just the time Mrs Hodsden left us that evening.'

'Precisely. Now, you told me on the 'phone that she'd been visiting at your house.'

'That's right.' Eagerly, with pathetic, transparent mendacity, he added, 'Visiting the wife.'

'Who is I believe an invalid.'

'That's it. Sees no one as a general rule. Not up to it. Any excitement and—whoof—she might go. That's what the doctor says.'

'Really? But Mrs Hodsden was a regular visitor, wasn't she?'

'Aye, that's right.' With that same fatal eagerness. 'Devoted. Twice weekly. Regular as clockwork.'

'No excitement from her, then.'

Corby squirmed. 'No. She was a marvellous sick visitor. Knew just the right tone to adopt. Soothing, like.'

'Really? Odd, I haven't had the impression of Mrs Hodsden as an exactly soothing figure.'

'Adaptable. Surprisingly adaptable,' said Corby, oozing another layer of sweat.

McHale sat back in his chair, a dangerous half-smile lurking in the corners of his thin mouth. 'Tell me, Mr Corby, is your wife's illness a mental one?'

'Mental? Good Lord no. Well, of course, it involves a lot of mental *suffering* . . .'

'It's just that your wife tells me that she never in her life set eyes on Mrs Hodsden.'

Corby exploded into a weak man's rage and shambled to his feet clutching his collar. 'Tells you? When—? How—?' He sank back in his chair, as if exhausted by all the tension. 'The bitch. How did she—?'

'Never mind that, Mr Corby. I think I'll do all the asking of questions. Perhaps you'd better decide to answer them truthfully this time, eh?'

Corby settled muttering in his chair, and looked at the inkwell, a picture on the wall, anywhere but into McHale's face. 'You'd no call to go behind my back and talk to her first,' he muttered, as if there were some obscure cricketing rules attached to police investigations.

'I'm very glad I did,' said McHale, that half-smile now more openly decorating his handsome, heavy face. 'Though frankly it doesn't seem as if your relations with Lill Hodsden were any great secret. Half the town seems to have known.'

'Oh, if you listen to the gossips—'

'Are you denying there were sexual relations between you?'

'Denying? 'Course I'm denying it. You've seen my wife: she's no companion to a man. Lill Hodsden came round to see me to chat—give me a bit of womanly sympathy.'

'Frankly, my impression is that womanly sympathy was no more Lill Hodsden's line than soothing invalids. You're not ringing true, Mr Corby.' McHale leaned forward and started raising his voice. 'You certainly paid well for this womanly sympathy, didn't you?'

'Paid? Who said anything about paying?'

'I did. I don't just mean money, either. That we might have difficulty tracing. But that colour TV—that'll be child's play to track back to you. And then there was talk of a car—'

'I bought her no bloody car.' Corby looked at his inquisitor with anguished indignation. 'If you ask me, a second-hand colour TV wasn't much to pay for all her kindness.'

'And if you ask me I'd say that brooch you gave her was a good deal too much.'

Corby jumped six inches out of his seat. 'Brooch? Who said anything about a brooch?'

McHale sighed, as if Corby were an antagonist un-

worthy of him. 'Mr Corby, I know you gave Lill
Hodsden a brooch from your wife's jewel-case not an
hour before she died.'

Wilf Hamilton Corby's pudgy, heavy face was bril-
liant with sweat by now, and he seemed on the verge
of crying. He began twisting his shoulders in anguish
as if trying to find a physical answer to the question
of which way to turn. 'Well—what if I did? It was
just a trinket—nearly worthless. *She's* never in a condition to wear them now.'

'How do I know it was worthless? Since it's disappeared we can't check that.'

'Disappeared?' Wilf Corby seemed outraged. Mc-
Hale kicked himself. He should have tested Corby to
see if he knew it was not on the body. As always with
lost opportunities in his investigations, he smoothed
it over, hid it even from himself.

'No doubt we can check that with your wife. She—
I suspect—will know exactly what was in the jewel-
box, and how much the missing piece was worth.'

'You'd believe her? Any old cracked bit of china's
a family heirloom if you listen to her. And she'd say
it was worth a fortune if she thought it'd land me
further in the shit.'

'She's been very helpful so far, at any rate. It
would save all of us a lot of trouble if you described
the brooch yourself.'

'Hardly noticed, tell you the truth. Just grabbed
something to calm her down. Sort of peacocky design
—bird, silver I think, glass in the eyes and the tail.
Dressy sort of stuff, if you know what I mean.'

'And you gave her this to—to calm her down.'
McHale leaned forward with a nasty sneer on his

face. 'Had you been getting her unnaturally excited, then?'

'Nothing to do with me.' Corby went scarlet, and for once in the interview McHale believed him. 'She arrived all het up. She'd had an argy-bargy with her daughter. Been sleeping with that black student or something. Makes your hair curl what girls will do these days, doesn't it? Then she'd met the bloke himself in the street, and had a showdown. He's the chap you ought to be grilling, you know. Anyway she was really put out when she arrived. Started going on about this and that—'

'Like getting you to marry her, for example?'

Corby let out a mystified yelp of anguish. 'Are you joking? With both of us married already?'

'It's easy enough these days. If you wanted to, it could have been arranged.'

'Who wanted to? I certainly didn't.'

'She wouldn't have been blackmailing you to make you more keen, would she?'

'Blackmail? What the hell would she have on me?'

'That,' said McHale, 'is something I shall be trying to find out.' He got up. 'Well, Mr Corby, I'm sorry to have to leave you dangling like this—'

'Wha'd'ye mean—dangling?'

'Uncertain, so to speak. Of course, if you were to act sensibly and come *completely* clean—'

'Wha'd'ye mean—completely clean? You've screwed my whole private life out of me—'

'Oh, I don't think so, Mr Corby. I really don't. I'm afraid we're going to have to follow this up very completely indeed if you don't come over with the complete story. You were, after all, the last man to

see Mrs Hodsden alive. Your wife says your affair
with her had lasted two years or more—'

'My wife! My God! What have I done to deserve a
woman like that? What did I do, marrying a treacher-
ous cow like her?'

McHale paused at the door and waved a hand at
the shipbuilding yard beyond. 'She brought you—all
this, didn't she, sir?'

He left Corby staring after him vindictively, with a
sense of having said something rather neat.

CHAPTER 15

TROUBLE AT THE HODSDENS'

McHale acted swiftly in the matter of Achituko, but in the event matters did not sort themselves out as quickly as he had hoped. Fetched from his lodgings at Mrs Carstairs's on Monday night by a peremptory pair of police constables (McHale chose the largest and thickest in Todmarsh), Achituko displayed admirable self-restraint and forbearance during the inquisition about his row with Lill Hodsden and his activities thereafter (by ten o'clock on the night of the murder he was sharing a chaste cup of Maltino with Eve Carstairs, but before that his doings were difficult to check). It was when the talk turned to his relationship with Debbie Hodsden, and in particular when the word 'deportation' was airily slotted into the conversation by McHale, that Achituko showed his metaphorical teeth and made it clear that he was no illiterate wog picked up on the streets without an entry permit and easy to bully into damaging admissions. He knew his rights, and stood on them; he knew English law, and he invoked it; he knew the techniques of opposition, and he used them. The thing developed into a duel between two obstinate personalities, and of the two Achituko was much the more subtle.

By Wednesday morning a stalemate had been reached. Achituko had mobilized on his side the Comparative Religions Department of the University of South Wessex, and McHale was having to face the prospect of figuring in a national civil rights scandal, with articles in the *New Statesman* and questions to the Home Secretary in Parliament. This was not how he had imagined achieving prominence in the larger national context. With a sigh he released Achituko into the custody of one of the defrocked clergymen on the staff of the Comparative Religions Department, on the understanding that he would not return to Todmarsh or attempt to make contact with Debbie Hodsden. Achituko enjoyed the duel and felt flattered by the friendly interest of his teachers at South Wessex. By the end of the week, though, he was finding the interest of the defrocked clergyman a good deal friendlier than he liked.

This was the news that McHale was able to give Gordon Hodsden when by chance he drove past him early on Tuesday evening, McHale on his way to talk to Guy Fawcett, Gordon out on his training run. Gordon bent over attentively at the window of the car, and when he got the details his saturnine face lit up with pleasure.

'Thanks,' he said, 'I appreciate what you've done.' And then he continued on his run.

As he jogged efficiently along the drab sea-front of Todmarsh he felt a warm, satisfying feeling in his bowels at a difficult job well done. Now Mum was gone, thank God, someone had to keep the family together. Fred's attempts to step into her shoes were ludicrous, as they all could see; and if it wasn't to be Fred, then who else could it be but he himself?

There wouldn't be any problem about that, aside from Debbie. Fred had always done as he was told, and would do so again, when he got used to the new regime. Brian was pretty docile, and might be expected to get a place at South Wessex in autumn, and do well. It was Debbie who was the green, useless sucker shooting from the Hodsden bush. She had gained an unruly independence during her years of fighting with Lill which was going to have to be knocked out of her. She complained she'd had to fight her own battles. Didn't everyone? Life didn't present you with your victories on a plate. Now that Achituko was gone, there could be a new start for Debbie: firm discipline, hard work, and something worthwhile and respectable when she left school. Something in an office, with good prospects. It would all work out all right if she was treated with a firm hand.

Gordon smiled. He was a young man who lived for the moment. Everything was beginning to look rosy for the future. His whole body felt suddenly relaxed from tension. He broke his training rules and turned, track-suited and sweating, into the Rose and Crown for a drink. His luck was in. Ann Watson was in there, for a casual hour's drink with a friend. Clutching his pint in his big carpenter's hands, he went over and sat down with them. They both welcomed him with smiles. Yes, the future was beginning to look brighter.

'OK, so I went into her house,' said Guy Fawcett, walking around his own front room, red-faced and blustering. 'So what? We were neighbours. Neighbours do drop in on each other. I know who told you about it, and you can take it from me, she's an evil-minded old woman.'

'She struck me, in fact, as an exceptionally truthful and observant person,' said McHale coolly.

'She'll be sorry she squealed to you, I can tell you that,' burst out Guy Fawcett, unwise in his agitation, and letting the bully show through.

'Are you threatening a witness?' asked McHale, raising his voice to an authoritative roar. 'I can assure you if you do that, it's *you* that will be sorry.'

'Just a joke,' muttered Fawcett, cringing. 'I can't stand these nosey-parkers.'

'The fact is, the pair of you were leading each other on, and then you went off into the house, with your arms round each other, and you doing God knows what with your hands. I suppose you'll say you were going to borrow a gardening book.'

Which put Guy Fawett into a quandry, because that was precisely what he had been going to say, and he couldn't for the life of him think of anything better.

When Ann Watson's friend had gone, Gordon began to feel for the first time that they were really getting on well together. No mystery about why. Now there was no reason why the subject of Lill should embarrass them. There was no reason why it should come up at all. Instead they sat at their little table, companionably, talking about the army, about being an army wife, about Northern Ireland.

'It's the women I'm sorry for,' said Gordon. 'Always was. I'd never have got married if I'd stayed in the army. No sort of life for them at all.'

'Oh, I quite liked it,' said Ann Watson, talking

freely with him because with his background he was one of the few people she knew who might understand. 'Of course there was the loneliness, and the separations, and you saw some of the wives going off the rails—but at least there wasn't any question of getting *stale*.'

'Most women would hate it,' said Gordon.

'Well, the army was his life, so it had to be part of mine. Some of my friends seemed to think I ought to be mildly ashamed of that, but I never was. The army's a job like any other . . . Of course, when he had a tour of duty in Northern Ireland, that was different . . . terrible.'

'Aye, it was that,' said Gordon, remembering. 'Still it wasn't so bad for us on duty. It made a man of you.'

'Oh?'

'You've no idea how quickly you grow up when you know the boy down the end of the alley may have a gun in his pocket. It makes you think—about yourself, about life. In the end, you're on your own in Northern Ireland: your mates can't help you much and you can't help them—all you can do is get a bit of your own back afterwards. When you've seen your mates blown up, you don't give a f—, you don't give a damn about the rules and the bloody procedures anymore. It's you against the rest, and you've just got your fists and your rifle.'

'Yes' said Ann sadly. 'I suppose that's how it gets you.'

Later, when he walked her home, Gordon tried to slip his arm around her, but she put it aside quite coolly: 'Don't.' But she talked away quite naturally, and listened when he told her about himself, about how rootless he felt, how uncertain about the future, lonely. Wasn't she lonely too?

'Yes, sometimes. But it's not really an unhappy feeling. Sometimes I almost like it.'

'But it must be difficult for you—just yourself and the child. And having a job too.'

'In a way. I wish I could care more about Beth. I wish I could give more of myself to her. She needs it, but I can't.'

They stopped by her gate, and Gordon put his hand on the post, loomed over her and kept her with him. 'You need to come out of yourself more. Get around a bit. You'd find it helped.'

'Everyone says that. But I don't think it would.'

'We could go out next weekend. There's a disco in Cumbledon. Would you come?'

'Oh, I don't think so. I used to love them, but that was years ago, and I was a different person.'

'Come on. It'd do us both good . . .' Gordon put his arms around her and very quickly drew her close to him. 'You know it's what we both need.'

'No—don't.'

'Come on. Relax. All I want's a kiss.'

'No no.' She pushed his chest and stooped from under to fumble with the latch of the gate. 'I'm sorry, Gordon.'

'Come on. Why won't you? You like me.' He caught her hands in his strong grip and pulled her back to face him. 'Admit it: you want me, don't you?'

'I like you,' she said gently. 'I don't want you.'

'*Why?* Tell me why?'

Ann Watson seemed to make a decision. 'It's funny. Sometimes . . . even at times like now . . . you just don't seem to be *there*.' She escaped into her front garden, and then seemed overcome with remorse. 'I expect it's something in me.'

Gordon swore loudly and charged off down the road.

'All right,' said Guy Fawcett at last, sweating—Mc-Hale thought he had been here before—but with a wry, lopsided grin on his face which was the prelude to an all-chaps-together act, 'I'll admit it: we had a bit of the old one-two. Heavens above, you're a man of the world. You can see what kind of a weed old Fred Hodsden is. Old Lill could eat up ten of him before breakfast and still be ready for more. She needed someone who knew what it was all about. And this wasn't the first time she'd marked down something she fancied and grabbed it with both hands, I can tell you.'

'I'm sure it wasn't,' said McHale with distaste written all over his face, side by side with the enjoyment. 'Unfortunate that in your case it happened to be only a couple of days before she was murdered, wasn't it?'

'Well, so what? Just a coincidence. We'd been eyeing each other off for weeks.'

'You're implying this was the first time, are you?'

' 'Course it was the first time. Ask old Mother Casey. We wouldn't have been going through the whole fandangle if it wasn't. Even that old battle-axe must have realized that.'

'Possibly. Or you could both have been putting on an act for her benefit.'

'We didn't know she was *there,* fer Chrissake. If we had it'd have been different, I can tell you. We'd have been round the front garden for a start. It was the first time—and the last.'

'Ah—so that was the kind of affair this was, was it? Just a once-off?'

'God, yes. I'd have seen to that.'

'Oh? You mean she'd have liked something more permanent?'

'Given half a chance.' Guy Fawcett swelled like an athletic bull-frog. 'I've got what it takes.'

'How interesting. Well now, let's recap on the situation: she was trying to nail you down, and you wanted out. Does that about sum things up?'

'No, no!' An expression of panic came over his face. 'I didn't mean that at all. I'm being misrepresented!'

'It sounded like that to me, sir. Perhaps we'd better go into this a little more closely.'

'Oh Christ,' muttered Guy Fawcett, regretting—not for the first time in his life—the too indiscriminate employment of his one great talent.

Gordon arrived back home in a foul mood. He felt the bile rising in him, and the urge for a fight—not a fight to liven up the day, such as Lill had enjoyed after a dull Sunday, but a fight to the kill, such as Lill had engaged in when she'd been thwarted.

Only Brian and Debbie were in—Fred having been emboldened to go out for the odd half pint for the third night running. Debbie, as usual, was crouched over a blockbuster, while Brian was watching some trendy media man condescending to the arts on BBC 2.

Inevitably it was Debbie who caught the full force of Gordon's mood. There had been only one thing in his day to give him any satisfaction, and he brought it out with a snarl of grim triumph.

'Well, I've settled your black stud's hash,' he said.

The unfamiliar word took a moment to get through

to Debbie, but when it did she flinched, and, raising her dark, dangerous eyes from her book said: 'What do you mean?'

'I say I've settled his hash. You won't be seeing him again.'

'I'm seeing him tomor—' She put her hands to her mouth.

'Oh, that was what you were planning, was it? Just as well I stepped in. Well, get this into your crazy skull: your little black Sambo's gone from Todmarsh for good. Before the end of the week he should be on his way back to Baboon land or where the hell he comes from. If he's not up on a charge of murder.'

'They can't send him back home. They've no right —he's studying here.'

'They've every right. There's immigration laws in this country, thank God, and they apply to students and all. There's other laws too—like about seducing a minor, for instance.'

'Oh, don't talk rot, Gordon. He didn't seduce me.'

'According to the law he did, or it'll be the same as if he did. I've been into all that. When they've finished going over him they'll put him on the first plane home. Got that? They'll deport him.'

As the idea got through to Debbie she let out suddenly a howl of rage and pain. 'They can't. Who's doing this? Is it that damned policeman?'

'Yes, it is. After I tipped him the wink.'

Screaming with anger and frustration. Debbie suddenly threw her book at his head and sprang at him herself in its wake. 'You beast! You bastard! I'll get you for this! I'll kill you!'

Sobbing and screaming she grabbed his hair and started clawing his face. Glad the thing had become a full-scale fight, fully confident at last, Gordon grabbed hold of her arms and started bending them back behind her. 'You bitch. You vile little bitch. You've met your match, little sister . . .' As her arms started to go limp and her face twisted in physical pain, Gordon relaxed, and still bending them back and up towards her shoulderblades, he started talking more softly: 'You're going to be grateful to me for this, you know. Later. When you know a bit more about life. You're going to see I was right . . .'

Now Debbie was sobbing with pain, and Brian said: 'Give over, Gordon. That's enough.' Slowly Gordon relaxed the pressure and Debbie collapsed on the floor in a racked, snuffling heap.

'You can't do this to me,' she gasped. 'I'm going to see that policeman.'

'Don't you try it, kid,' said Gordon, standing over her in gladiatorial triumph. Quick as a flash Debbie seized one of his ankles and half-toppled him over one of the easy chairs. Then, on her feet in an instant, she made for the door. Gordon, righting himself, caught her just as she was going out of the front door, dragged her back into the hall and banged her head against the wall.

'Oh, little sister,' he shouted, 'you've got so much to learn. Do you want to learn it the hard way?'

Next door, with Guy Fawcett squirming and twisting on the end of his inquisitorial line, Inspector McHale heard the shouting and the banging on the wall from the Hodsden house. He raised his eyebrows imperceptibly. The happy Hodsden family . . . He

hadn't expected them to break out like this. Perhaps
he ought to go and investigate.

But that very moment there came through from
the Station the 'phone call that was to change the
whole course of the investigation.

CHAPTER 16

CONFESSION

It was what McHale had half expected all along. In fact it was what he had hoped for. He had alerted his colleagues in the Cumbledon police, and they had contacted him immediately it had come up.

The boy sat in the charge-room, a heavy lad of nineteen or so, his manner poised between bluster and terror. If his body—incipiently mountainous and ugly—might arouse fear, his face could only arouse contempt: large-headed, dim, inarticulate, his mouth always in danger of falling open, he was the typical rural lout who in this urban age finds himself a place among the dregs of the towns. His face was spotty and pockmarked, his eyes shifty and wet; he wore a cheap plasticated leather jerkin, zipped to the throat and sewn over with incomprehensible badges, and filthy jeans. He smelt. Even as McHale entered the room he involuntarily wrinkled his nostrils. A sensitive policeman, McHale.

'Well, you've landed yourself right in it,' he said.

'I ain't done nothing,' muttered the boy feebly.

But what he had done was all-too-well attested to. Earlier that evening, at dusk—he had not even had the wit to wait until it was completely dark, so keen was he to pick up a few pounds and buy himself a drink, and perhaps a piece of skirt—he had attacked an old lady limping home along one of the back alleys of Cumbledon. Watched from behind the curtains of one of the little cottages that lined the alley, he had grabbed the woman's handbag and hit her efficiently with a homemade cosh. But the old lady was fragile, and when she was found two minutes later she was dead. And when this boy was picked up ten minutes later he was scrabbling in her purse, which he threw away under the eyes of the police patrol that took him. Crumpled in his hand was £1.75. When told that the old lady was dead, he said: 'She can't be. I didn't hit her hard.' He was a boy who seemed destined from birth to a lifetime of shorter or longer jail sentences. By bad luck he was likely to start with a stiff one.

McHale settled himself, comfortably yet intimidatingly, on another upright chair on the boy's side of the desk.

'What's your name?'

'Jack Cobbett. I told the other one.'

'It's me you're dealing with now. Where do you live?'

'Furmety Lane.' It was a tatty, slummy district in East Cumbledon that even the coming of university people to the town (which had transformed many undesirable areas into estate agents' dreams) had failed to make habitable except by those who couldn't help it.

'What does your father do?'

'He's with the Council. On the roads.'

'Mother?'

'Yer.'

'Does your mother work?'

'On and off. Cleaning and that. When she can't get anything better. She won't care.'

'So I gather. She's been informed.'

'Coulder told you she wouldn't care. She never has. Ran off with a bloke when I was thirteen.'

'Ah. You hold it against her?'

'Wish she'd never bloody come back.'

'You've got a grudge against your mother?'

'No . . . Just can't stand the sight of her.'

'Interesting. Well, what she actually said when she was told was: "I seen it coming. He can stew in his own juice." '

The boy was silent, his face impassive. 'What am I supposed to do? Cry?'

'I'm interested. Why do you attack women? Are you getting your own back for being deserted?'

'Don't be bloody daft,' muttered Jack Cobbett.

'There must be some reason why you choose women . . .'

'Women are bloody weaker—' burst out Jack. 'Don't be f— daft.'

'Older women too, not younger. There was the one tonight, and then the one in Todmarsh: she was nearly fifty. About your mother's age.'

'What the bleeding hell do you mean? Todmarsh.'

'Nearly fifty. Not unlike your mother too, I'd guess.'

'I never been near Todmarsh.'

'Never been there? Are you really telling me that? Todmarsh on the coast, and Cumbledon being inland?'

'Well, I been there . . . in my time.'

'Of course you have. Silly to tell unnecessary lies. You were there last Thursday, for example.'

'The hell I was.'

'Where were you last Thursday then? Thursday night.'

'Thursday night? How would I know? One night's like any other.'

'Not this night. You'd better think carefully.'

The boy, sweating now, cradled his big head in his hands. The long, thick, strong fingers picked convulsively at his dirty, lifeless hair. McHale looked at him, looked at the hands. Strangler's hands, he thought.

'I was at the flicks with a bird,' said Jack Cobbett at last. 'One I picked up. Casual.'

'What did you see?'

'Don't remember ... *The Stud.*'

'*The Stud* was on the week before last. You were in Todmarsh Thursday evenng, weren't you?'

'Sod off. I told you. I haven't been there for years.'

'You were there last week. And you wanted the odd pound for a drink, didn't you? Just like tonight.'

'I didn't do nothing tonight.'

'You were caught with the money on you so don't try giving me that stuff. You were seen to throw away the dead woman's purse. You had a receipt with her name on when we picked you up.'

The boy was near to blubbering. 'It's a bloody frame-up. I didn't have no receipt.'

'What's more, you were seen from the house when you attacked the poor old creature. By someone who knew you. It's an open-and-shut case. Hardly worth the bother of a trial. They're just getting the details of the charge ready out there.'

Jack Cobbett choked and spluttered. 'It's a frame-

up. I never . . .' His big shoulders began to heave
with fear and nausea. 'I didn't know . . .'

'You didn't know your own bloody strength, is that
it? I'm not so sure about that. You'd enough practice.
Did you go for an OAP this time because you wanted
an easy victim? You had more of a struggle last time,
eh?'

'There wasn't no last time, I tell you.'

'She wasn't so weak, that one, was she? A real
tough bird I should think.'

'You're bloody making this up. You'll be saying I
did the Great Train Robbery next.'

'No, just another mugging, like this one. You had
us fooled for a bit there, Jack. Quite a neat job. How
much did you get out of that one?'

'You're talking a load of balls.'

'More than one seventy-five, I bet. And then there
was the brooch.'

'What brooch? What are you talking about?'

'The brooch you took off her dress. What did you
do with it, eh? Get anybody to take it off you? Did you
give it to a bird? Or did you throw it away? Pity if you
did that. It was a valuable little piece.'

He looked for signs of disappointment, but saw
nothing but bullish vacancy.

'Either way,' he said flatteringly, 'you managed
that little job better than the one tonight, didn't
you? Nice dark little patch you found. No one to see
you. And Mrs Hodsden trotting down the road. Did
she remind you of your mum? She's got bright red
hair. What colour's your mum's hair?'

'She's a bleeding blonde.'

'Dyed, I suppose. Out of a bottle?'

'What do you think? She's no bleeding Swede.'

'Just like Lill Hodsden. Bit of the tart there, eh? And you'd got your bit of wire there, hadn't you? Nice little instrument, I'd guess . . . with handles all prepared, eh? Just wanted to frighten her, didn't you?'

'I don't know what you're talking about,' said the boy, still half way between a snarl and a whimper.

'But when you got it round her neck you found you wanted to go on, didn't you? You found you liked it, that was it, wasn't it? Enjoyed it. Did you have an erection while you were doing it, eh, Jack?'

'Here—'

'And before you knew where you were she was on the ground dead, wasn't she? What did you do with the wire, Jack?'

Jack was breathing hard, and sweating, and snivelling on and off. 'You're talking in bloody riddles,' he whined.

'Oh, I'm not. You know what I mean, don't you? You took her purse, didn't you? And the brooch. And then you made off. What did you do with the wire? Did you go and throw it in the sea? Or have you still got it at home? Ready for next time?'

'You go and look. I ain't got nothing there.'

'Because there would have been a next time, wouldn't there? You got such a kick out of that little job. It felt as if it was someone else's neck in that wire, didn't it?'

'Give over—'

'Someone you wanted very much to do in, and didn't dare, eh?' McHale leant his face very close to the boy's crouching figure and his panting, distorted face: 'Why don't you admit it? Come clean. It'll help you in the long run.'

The boy whimpered miserably. 'Oh, all right. I did it. That job tonight. I didn't mean her to snuff it. God's truth.'

'Oh, we all know about that business tonight. No mystery about that. What I'm interested in is the Todmarsh one.'

'There wasn't one. I didn't—'

'Oh yes you did. Last Thursday. What did you think when you saw her, walking down the road? There was you in this dark little recess, and there was this woman, walking down the road. Big, sexy woman she was, wasn't she? Reminded you of your mother . . .'

'What's my bleeding mother got to do with it?'

'Quite a lot, Jack. Quite a lot. I don't suppose you intended much harm when you put the wire round her neck, did you? That's what you can say at the trial, anyway, and we won't go against that, not if you cooperate. We're not against you, Jack. We just want to clear this thing up.'

Jack was whining noisily all the time now. 'You've got it in for me . . .'

'We haven't, Jack. We just want to know how it happened. You tightened the wire, didn't you? You're a strong lad, Jack. Tighter and tighter—'

'No!'

'And she was gasping, and choking, wasn't she?—'

'No! No!'

'Tighter and tighter. And you could feel her body under you go limp. And still you kept pulling it, tighter and tighter—'

'No! Yes! No! Yes . . . yes . . . yes . . .'

CHAPTER 17

HAPPY ENDING

And that was the end of the Hodsden case. As a case.
And it had all worked out as McHale had prophesied
—and publicly prophesied at that. He drew Inspector
Haggart's attention to the fact when he cleared up
his things at the Todmarsh Police Station.

'You remember I said as much at the time,' he
said, congratulating himself with the air of pinning
a medal on to someone else. 'It's often the way: these
casual muggings lead to killings, and they're the very
devil to clear up. Can't do much more than wait for
the bastard to do it again.'

'The boy confessed, didn't he?'

'Oh yes,' said McHale, stacking his papers into a
neat pile and sliding them into his brief-case. 'Of
course, now he's got himself a lawyer—at your and my
expense—and he's taken it all back. Just to make
things difficult. But he confessed all right, and signed
on the dotted line.'

'Did you trace the money, or the brooch?'

'Not yet. We'll have to, if we're going to make any
sort of a case. But luckily that's not vital. We've got
a cast-iron case on him with this poor old thing he
did in Cumbledon last night. Vicious little bugger.
Makes me livid.'

Inspector Haggart, standing there in the evening sunlight, thought for a bit. 'Funny the two different weapons,' he said. 'That garrotte thing, and then the cosh. Suggests two different kinds of crime. Two different personalities.'

'Well, naturally he wouldn't use the wire again, not the next time,' said McHale impatiently. 'He's dim, but he's not defective.'

'Do you see any pattern in these things, then?' asked Haggart, with an appearance of deferring, since this seemed the best strategy with McHale.

'Oh yes, I think so. I thought so the moment I heard from one of the sergeants over there what kind of woman his mother was. Same type as Lill Hodsden, that was clear. Ran off with a truck-driver when the boy was thirteen. Came back, but there it is—the damage was done. These killings are a sort of revenge on his mother. These women are surrogate victims, killed because of his love/hate for his mother. He's revenging himself for his feelings of desertion and neglect.'

McHale was not an unintelligent man. If he had thought a little he might have come up with something better than this Freud-and-pap. But McHale did not cultivate his intelligence. He cultivated his career. And of course he'd seen how this case would end all along.

'Interesting case,' said Inspector Haggart, non-committally. He was a genuinely intelligent man, though it had never got him very far. He seemed to be the kind of man who always said things his superior officers did not want to hear. Now he said: 'I misunderstood. I thought you said the woman in Cumbledon was a "poor old thing".'

McHale shot him a look. 'Well?'

'Hardly the same type as Lill Hodsden. Or as the mother, by the sound of it.'

McHale drew his already thin lips still more closely around his teeth. 'It was nearly dark. Late evening. That's a minor detail. I tell you, if we can trace the brooch back to him, we've got a case. If we don't find it, we'll come down on him heavy as we know how on the Cumbledon killing. He's in for a long stretch, that thug. As far as we're concerned, the case is closed.'

The case was closed. Everybody satisfied. Happy ending.

Well, McHale was happy anyway. He did not see the look on Inspector Haggart's face that followed him as he stalked out of the room. It was a look that was to be reproduced quite often in his later career, on the faces of both his superiors and his inferiors in the police force. But McHale did not see it, and felt happy. The case was closed.

He used almost the identical phrase again when talking to Fred Hodsden about the outcome of the investigation, a little later in the day.

'You can rest assured, Mr Hodsden,' he said, speaking earnestly to cover the contempt he felt, standing in the Hodsden living-room (now so bare of ornament) but poised for flight as soon as the decent civilities were over, 'that this young thug is the man who did it. That'll be a weight off your mind, I'm sure. And if we can't bring your wife's murder home to him, then we'll throw the book at him over the Cumbledon one. It's good to be able to tell you at last that the case is all sewn up.'

Fred breathed a sigh of relief. 'You've done a grand

job, Inspector. A right down grand job. The kids
and I can rest in peace now.'

And that evening, down at the Yachtsman (for
Fred went out much more often of a night, now) Fred
said to his mates: 'They're a grand body of men, the
police. Brains like razors. You don't want to believe
what you read in them Sunday newspapers. You
wouldn't hope to meet anyone sharper or straighter
than that McHale.'

And everyone round the table nodded, because isn't
that what everyone wants to believe?

So the case was closed. Everyone in Todmarsh accepted that, though one or two (such as Miss Gaitskell,
who had poured sherry and information into the
Chief Inspector, and had her own ideas on the matter) were a mite surprised at the outcome. It was now
no longer a matter of uncertainty how to treat the
Hodsdens—they fell neatly back into place: they were
a brave, bereaved little family, not quite up to par
socially. Everyone behaved accordingly.

So everything was quite satisfactory. A happy ending. Well, happyish. Happy endings only occur in
books, and then only in books written long ago. But
certainly the Hodsden family settled down into a
peaceful enough routine. Brian got his scholarship
levels, not brilliantly, and got a holiday job in a book-
shop over the summer. He and Gordon sometimes
went out together in the long warm evenings. They
acquired a taste for good food, and sampled the three
or four better restaurants in Cumbledon, turn and
turn about. They talked about a holiday in Italy next
year.

I should feel free, thought Brian often. Eventually
I will feel free.

So they were both busy, especially as Gordon was running an intricate love-life at the same time. Brian wondered at the number of the girls he had, and speculated that the murder had rendered him even more attractive. But he never went out with Ann Watson, never. In spite of the bustle of their lives, both the boys were good to Gran next door. Mrs Casey was at the same time vigorous and failing. She gave her opinions as unsparingly as ever, but sometimes now those opinions did not seem to make sense. Her mind seemed more lurid than ever with hell-fire and burning rocks, though she still enjoyed her creature comforts.

At home Gordon was able to rule with an easier rein. Fred was off out most evenings, and that was all right by Gordon. If he would never do them any credit, equally he would never disgrace them. Everyone would have said it was a happy ending for Fred—though Fred himself would have denied it, and said that he missed Lill painfully. Debbie too was quiet enough. The strong-arm tyranny of Gordon's early days in command seemed to have paid off. She rarely disobeyed him, perhaps thinking him, in comparison with Lill, the lesser of two evils.

Debbie then was happy? Perhaps. And broken in? Hmm. Did Debbie Hodsden give you the impression of being easily broken in?

A busy, sunny, active (especially for Gordon) summer shaded gracefully into autumn. Brian started at the University of South Wessex, doing History. The History Department was not a very good one: it was staffed by trendy publicists who spent their time reviewing unread books for *Kaleidoscope,* with a sprinkling of incompetent youngsters engaged because they were cheap. Still, Brian began to make new friends, to get himself into a circle. Not a fast set, but a quiet, cosy circle. All in all he was not unhappy though he was now and then listless, now and then restless.

So that's how things worked themselves out for the Hodsdens. And things were just as predictable for all the other men and women who crossed Lill Hodsden's path in the last week of her mortal life. Perhaps we could take the sphere of their lives and slice it through at one day, just to see how they are getting on. Let's say, at random, Saturday October 18th.

On Saturday October 18th, nearly six months after Lill's death, most of the people who knew her best were by coincidence, in Cumbledòn. There was a disco-dance at the University Union, the biggest event so far in the student term. A group called Scarlett O'Hara was coming over from Bristol. Brian hadn't intended going along, but Gordon had urged him, and it had ended with his taking Gordon along as his guest. Oddly enough, he felt decidedly proud of Gordon. Gordon had force, even a sort of magnetism—which his student friends certainly did not have, though they recognized it in him. He had lived, where they were merely peering cautiously over the tops of their nests. What was more, he knew how to behave with them: if the conversation went above his head, he had the sense not to try and join in it, and was equally impressive silent.

He went down well with the girls, that was for sure. Practically the whole of the student population was there, as well as a sprinkling of staff, and the clothes ranged from sequins to sackcloth just as the behaviour ranged from courtly to rural. As the evening wore on and the boys of Scarlett O'Hara played wilder and wilder (going periodically behind the scenes for something or other) Gordon spread himself around (his big, looming body tastefully, almost conventionally dressed, with a stupendous splash of colour in the tie) first among the three or four rather dim little girls that had come along with Brian and his group, then with some who had caught his eye, then—it seemed—making joyous efforts to dance with the entire female part of the university. He even danced with a Professor of Microbiology, *and* took her off to a dark corner afterwards.

Back in Todmarsh three of the circle who had known, or known of, Lill Hodsden and perhaps would have liked to murder her were at home. Ann Watson put her daughter to bed, marked some exercise books, made herself cocoa, all in a dream, from which she would not wake for years yet. Drusilla Corby, alone, sat before the television in her living-room having got up as soon as her husband left the house. Made up to the nines, in a sequined evening gown from the late 'fifties, she hugged a whisky bottle to herself. This was the life! She should have done this before! One of these days she might actually go out. Lill Hodsden's death, somehow, seemed to have liberated her.

She took another swig. And though it was only an old movie, and an old Bob Hope movie at that, she sat there on the sofa, giggling helplessly, perfectly happy.

Not half a mile away, at home and in her own bed, Mrs Casey lay—as so often nowadays—not wakeful, but hideously torn between consciousness and sleep, racked with dreams that seemed not so much dreams as visions of hideous prophecy. She went to bed early these days, but her nights were always thus, and her mornings hag-ridden. Once she had been near to asking her doctor for a prescription for sleeping tablets, but she had finally put aside any such display of human weakness. So she tossed, and turned, and moaned, and sometimes there would ring out from the sleeping form some phrase or other, some fragment drawn from her reading. She cried one now:

'And the dogs shall eat Jezebel . . . all but the skull and the feet and the palms of her hands.'

Her forehead wrinkled in puzzlement in her sleep.

In a tiny, nasty cinema in Cumbledown, once a section of a large, nasty cinema, part of a chain, Guy Fawcett went through the usual motions with a seventeen-year-old dolly bird he'd bought for a whisky and ginger ale and the price of admission. He grunted and she giggled and the ten or twelve other people in the cinema shifted uneasily in their seats.

'I think you're wonderful,' the witless creature said breathlessly. 'So *virile*. Will you buy me a vodka and Coke afterwards?'

Guy's life seemed to have reverted to normal. Guy was happy.

About quarter to eleven, still tirelessly dancing, it occurred to Gordon to wonder about Debbie. And being Gordon he had to do something about it. When the music ended for a moment he excused himself and went over to the table where Brian was sitting alone with Eric, one of his new university friends. Gordon said: 'I think I'll ring Mrs Dawson, see Debbie's all right.'

Mrs Dawson was mother of Debbie's friend Karen, with whom she was spending the night.

Brian felt a bit embarrassed at this display of old-time patriarchy on the part of his brother and in front of his friend. 'Oh don't, Gordon. You'll make her ashamed. It'll look as if you're checking up on her.'

'Well, I am. No reason to be ashamed if she's not doing anything.'

And Gordon swung off confidently in the direction of the telephones. Brian turned to Eric in renewed intimacy.

'It's since Mother died,' he said. 'Gordon feels he's responsible for the family. He's a good chap.'

'Great,' agreed Eric, a fair, stocky lad from Torquay. 'Still, you don't want to let him overdo it.'

'Overdo it?'

'This head of the household business. After all, you've got to lead your own life, haven't you?'

'Oh yes, of course,' agreed Brian readily. But a sudden wave of depression came over him. Would he ever lead his own life? *Could* he? After a while Gordon came back, happy again.

'Did you talk to her?'

'No, she was out with the dog for a last walk. But Mrs Dawson said it was all right.'

In a little coppice on the farthest extreme of the University's grounds (sold to the fledgling body in 1960 by a squireling at a sum so exorbitant that he was still busy squandering the money at casinos in the South of France) Debbie Hodsden lay ecstatically happy under a body much larger than her own, enjoying pleasures all the sweeter for having been in abeyance for some months.

'Aren't you afraid of your brother finding out?' the body said.

'He won't,' giggled Debbie. 'I've got Mrs Dawson squared. She thinks he's a tryant, and she said she'd lie for me. He'll never find out, not Gordon. Give Mum her due: she was a good deal brighter than our Gordon.'

The other body muttered with satisfaction, and pressed himself closer in his pleasure. The leg of his trousers, protruding from the coppice, slid up over his sock. The skin underneath it was smooth, gleaming, and black.

Wilf Hamilton Corby, in a cosy little semi-detached on the outskirts of Cumbledon, was enjoying a companionable glass of something strong with a widow he had met by answering an advertisement. 'Companionship,' it had said, was the end in view. And certainly he seemed to find her soothing. She listened very well indeed, and rarely tried to tell him about herself.

'Of course, I'm the last one to complain,' he was saying, 'but being tied to an invalid wife all these years has been no joke.'

'I'm sure it hasn't,' said his widow.

'Particularly one of her disposition,' said Wilf resentfully.

'Tell me about her,' said the widow.

And Wilf got down to doing just that. Odd that he hadn't noticed the determined set of the widow's jaw, or the glint of contempt for him in her eyes. Had he done so, might he not have thought of frying pans and fires?

* * *

Watching Gordon out on the dance floor again, still smart and precise in his dress, yet spreading his vitality around him like shock treatment, Brian found himself unable to throw off that slight cloud of depression. All that energy, that zest, that animal enjoyment of life.

'I wish—' he said.

'What?' said his friend Eric, bending close.

'I wish . . . looking at Gordon, out there, dancing . . . He's so alive, so . . . electric. He's got something I haven't got. I wish . . . I wish I could give pleasure like that . . . or feel it.'

'I expect you will one day,' said Eric, looking at him.

'When I go out there . . . and dance with a girl . . . I can't do it, not with my whole body, not like Gordon. It doesn't do anything to me. Look at him now. That girl, she's quite an ordinary girl, but Gordon's all bright, like she was plugging him into the mains . . . I never feel like that.'

'That's because you're different, made different,' said Eric.

And with a strange, secret shock of pleasure Brian felt Eric's hand, under the table, reach out for his, and take it in his own warm one, comfortingly.

Eve Carstairs, at a business dinner-dance with her husband, danced the last waltz, holding him closely to her. He was pot-bellied, tired, resentful of her energy, but she closed her eyes and transformed him in her mind into something else again—taller, stronger, younger, and of quite another colour.

* * *

Fred Hodsden, drinking his last half pint after the
darts tournament he had helped to win (his game
was much improved these days, by practice) sank
into a sea of well-being and became quite loquacious,
for Fred. He talked about Lill, what a wonderful
mother she'd been, how he'd like to flay alive the
young bastard who did it, and what a wonderful
little family he'd got, thanks to Lill.

'I'd best be getting back, soon as you're ready,' he
said, looking around the team. 'The boys are at a
dance, but I reckon they'll be home and wanting their
suppers before long.' He sighed contentedly. 'It's a
big responsibility, bringing up a family on your
own.'

'You should be looking about you now, Fred,' said
one of his mates. 'You're the marrying type.'

'Aye,' said Fred. 'I'd thought of that.'

'I need the loo,' said Brian, after he and Eric had
sat at the table, silent amid the din, for a very long
time. It had seemed there was no group, no ampli-
fiers, no dancers. Only a still world, suddenly remade.

'So do I,' said Eric. 'I'll join you.'

They made for the door, but Brian said nervously:
'I expect Gordon will be back soon.'

'What if he is?' said Eric. Brian, as though treading on uncertain ground, cast his eyes back nervously
at the dance floor, at the bright clothes and the drab,
at the sweaty faces red from drink, the matt faces
glazed from drugs, those vile bodies. He could see no
Gordon among them.

'Come on,' said Eric softly, and he pulled himself
through the door.

Out in the corridor they avoided by silent consent the big lavatory nearest the Student Union hall, by now probably vile with spew or worse. They walked along corridors, up stairways, into alcoves, until the music receded to nothing and there seemed to be only themselves suspended over nothing, with something drawing them together they hardly understood and could not talk about. Finally they found a little gents in the corner of the Russian department, totally deserted, quiet as the grave. They went in. They had reached the ultimate bourne of so many predecessors of their kind, the little-frequented public loo.

They pissed, looking everywhere but down or at each other, and then they went over to the washbasin. They looked, not at each other but at each other in the mirrors: they looked over-bright in the harsh fluorescent glare, tensed up for something to happen. As Brian put his hand down to turn on the tap Eric took it again, openly, tenderly, and drew Brian around to face him. After a moment he drew him closer, closer . . .

The door opened and they shot apart.

'Oh Gordon—'

Gordon walked over to the latrines with a false casualness.

'Oh hello, Brian. Just the chap I wanted to talk to. Been looking all over.' Eric and Brian stood awkward in the over-bright light, unable to do anything but watch. Gordon finished and zipped himself up. 'I said I wanted to talk to my brother,' he repeated.

'Can't you—?'

'GET!'

Eric looked at Brian, and then at Gordon. Then as Gordon took two menacing steps forward he scooted through the door. They heard his footsteps echoing down the corridor. Gordon continued his walk forward, and when he got to the basins, with a sudden lithe movement he caught his brother under the collar and jerked his head back against the mirror.

'You bloody little fool!'

'Gordon—'

'You bloody little fool! You need cooling off! I've a good mind to put your head under this tap.'

'Stop it, Gordon. You're choking me.'

'I would too. Christ, you make me sick. I never thought I'd see my brother playing monkey tricks like that. Handy-pandy under the table with another adolescent queer.'

'It was the first time!'

'And the fucking last!'

'Nobody saw us.'

'I saw you!'

'Nobody would care. What's it to them? People's private lives are their own these days. Nobody thinks about it like that anymore.'

'I THINK ABOUT IT LIKE THAT! Get that message, boy. Do you think I want a pansy for a brother?'

'You're just old-fashioned.'

'Thank Christ I am. Do you think I don't know about your sort? We had them in the army all right, don't you worry. Officers. Offer you a drink all friendly, and the next thing you know they're feeling your crotch. Oh no, little brother. I'm not having anyone in our family joining the fairy-queen set.'

'Give over, Gordon. Let me go. We'll talk about it in the morning.'

But Gordon was not going to be temporized with, and kept his large hand firmly on the neck of Brian's shirt.

'We're talking about it now. Are you getting the message? You'd better be. Because you're going to swear to me that this is the last time you try any of those grubby little tricks.'

'Oh, don't talk rot, Gordon. I'm nineteen. I'm not under your thumb. I'm at university. Soon I'll be out working. I'm not going to swear away my life just because you're so bloody medieval.'

'You're going to do just what I tell you to. I can see I was wrong just to worry about Debbie. All the time there was you, itching to play arse bandits with your little palsy-walsy. Well, get the message, boy: I'm in charge of the Hodsden family now. And if I find you playing these little games again, I'll take you apart, I'll half murder you.'

'Don't be so bloody melodramatic, Gordon.'

'You think it's just wind, do you? Well, it wouldn't be the first time. There was a boy in Northern Ireland. I suspected him of shopping one of my mates to the Provos.' Gordon forced Brian down on to the washbasin and stood over him, twisting his tie, and looking at him intently with a glowering, remembering gaze. 'I got hold of that boy, and I took him, in my army truck, way way out of town and when I'd finished with him his own mother couldn't bear to look at him . . . I worked on him for three hours, slowly . . . He'll never walk again . . . So don't think this is just big talk, baby brother. I'd do it to you if I thought you were disgracing us.'

'You're making this up. You'd've told me . . .'

'There are some things you flabby intellectuals are too soft to hear. You think you know about life, don't you, but you know *nothing*.'

'I know I'm nineteen. I know I can leave home and come into residence here whenever I want. I know you've got no legal hold over me.'

'That's typical. That's your sort of knowledge. Legal knowledge. Book knowledge. Well, this is my gut knowledge: I've got all the hold I need. In fact I've got you by the short hairs.'

'Oh yes? How?'

'I've got the hold that you and me, together, planned the murder of our late departed mum, Lill Hodsden, who was duly murdered on April 24, 19—'

Brian laughed with relief and almost forgot the hard hand at his throat. 'Some hold! Who's going to care about that? That boy in Cumbledon's been tried.'

'Not for Lill's murder. It wouldn't matter even if he had. Cases can be reopened. They'd still be interested if I went along.'

'Went along and what? Said that, lying in our bedroom, we talked about the murder of our mother—? Don't talk rot.'

'Which murder duly took place in the manner we had planned it, strangulation, by a piece of wire, strong, thick wire now lying buried in the War Memorial Gardens—'

'They never found the wire—'

'Where one day next Spring, perhaps, old Fred will turn it over with his rake and throw it on the rubbish heap—'

'Old Fred?'

'—without thinking it's the wire that sent his better

half to judgment, because the handles aren't there, the handles were twisted off it, and thrown on the fire of the Rose and Crown, in the Saloon Bar, at ten to ten on the night of the murder, where they burned away to nothing.'

'Gordon! You're lying!' Brian struggled free and looked at his brother. The vital body that had seemed so full of energy on the dance floor now seemed to crackle with violent force as Gordon remembered back to the night in April. When the full realization of what he was saying struck Brian, he keeled over towards the washbasins and retched.

'Oh, you throw up at the thought, don't you? I knew you were too weak to go through with it. Do you think I didn't feel like throwing up? I held it back. All the way back to the pub I held it back. I drank beer with the rest—poured it down while I was churning up inside. It was only after we'd heard, on the way up—'

'Stop it, Gordon, for God's sake! I don't believe you. You're just saying it because that's what you *wanted* to do.'

'Wanted to do and did. I could see you were chickening out. You were never really on in the first place, were you? And as soon as Mum and Debbie had that fight you were going to use it, weren't you, as your little get-out? You're a gutless little weed. So I had to take it all on myself. I just changed the day, changed the venue, then went ahead and did it. I enjoyed it, too.'

'You didn't—'

'I did. I enjoyed feeling her body under me. I enjoyed seeing her looking at me. I put my head out

into the light, just for a second so she could see, and
know. She knew it was me. She knew I was murdering her. That's what I enjoyed most of all.'

'You're lying, Gordon. Romancing. Just to make
yourself feel big.'

Quick as a flash Gordon dived into the inside pocket
of his suit and came out with something cradled in
the palm of his hand. 'Remember that brooch? The
one the Inspector was after, to get a lead on that boy?
The one Corby had given her? What do you think
this is?'

He opened his palm and shoved his hand under
Brian's eyes. Sparkling in the over-bright light was a
little silver peacock, with diamonds studding its head
and tail—a worthless, expensive trinket, Lill's last love-
offering.

'Lovely, isn't it? Real class. It's been hidden at work.
If they'd found it they'd have suspected old Corby.
I'm going to keep it on me always. To remind me
of my finest hour. Tell me I'm alive.'

Brian's eyes, glazed and disbelieving, stared at the
jewel, winking hypnotically in the white light. The
brooch from Lill's dress, the brooch that had been
ripped off the body. Suddenly he felt stunned,
crushed: there was no more room for doubt. Again
he keeled over, and sobbed and retched into the washbasin till he felt empty of everything except fear.

'So you see,' said Gordon, silky of voice, when at
last Brian forced himself upright and cooled his forehead against the icy mirror, 'here we are, both in
this together. Just as we planned. You—at the very
least—as accessory before the fact. So get this straight:
if I go and confess, you're in it with me.'

'You wouldn't confess. Why would you?'

'I don't know,' said Gordon, suddenly thoughtful, almost sad. 'Sometimes I feel like it. Sometimes I feel there . . . there isn't any point to things. Any meaning anymore. Do you know what . . . she . . . what Ann said to me? She said: "When I'm with you, it's as though, somehow, you're not *there*." ' He swallowed, as if he had crunched a nasty pill. 'I know what she meant, now. Mum did that to us. To you too. She sucked us dry, and spat out the pips. These girls I've been fucking all summer. Do you know why there've been so many? Because they're not interested after they've been with me two or three times. I expect they feel the same. That's how she left us, our Lill. Really all I've got is the family . . .'

Brian did not speak, a terrible fear on him.

'You. And Debbie. Even old Fred. It's something. Something I've got to do. My responsibility. And I'm going to make a job of it. We're not going to be the town laughing-stocks, like we were. You're none of you going to disgrace us.'

Brian could stand it no more. 'I've got my life to live, Gordon,' he wailed. 'My life!'

His tone of desperation seemed to wake Gordon out of his depression. He shook off his mood like a dog reaching dry land.

'No, *we*'ve got *our* lives to live. We're all together in this, even more so since she died. I'm never going to get Ann. Perhaps I never expected to. Perhaps what I did it for was so the family would have a future. So I could knock it into shape. And I will too. This mood of mine, it'll pass. Things will get better. All we need is a bit of discipline. You'll be a credit to us. Debbie will come to something. I'll keep you on the right lines.'

'Gordon, I don't want to be kept on your lines. I don't want you to take responsibility for me.'

'You've no choice. That's what I did it for. I've got to make it worthwhile in the long run.'

'Gordon, I didn't want that. I didn't want her dead.'

Gordon squared his shoulders and took his brother by the arm.

'I know. That's why I did it alone. I had to set you free. I did it for you, baby brother. I did it for you.'

Brian looked bleakly ahead, in the bright white light of the washroom, and saw nothing but the shadow of another tyranny looming before him.